MANNERS AND MURDER
(A Carolina Pennsbury Mystery)

by

Helen Grochmal

For information, email **Cozy Cat Press**, cozycatpress@aol.com or visit our website at: www.cozycatpress.com

COZY CAT
PRESS

ISBN: 978-1-939816-24-5

Printed in the United States of America

Cover design by Nicole Spence
www.covershotdesigns.com

1 2 3 4 5 6 7 8 9 10

Thank you to Felicia and Sherida Yoder for their editing help, but especially for their many years of friendship.

CHAPTER ONE—VIEW OF A ROUND TABLE

Lear should not have retired. That is when all of the troubles began in Britain at the time. The people in the retirement home should have learned from Lear. They didn't, so there was that trouble that wouldn't have happened if they had all been at work or busy in their own homes. In some ways, Carolina's personality was a lot like Cordelia's if Cordelia had lived to old age, especially in wanting to be a peacemaker and a keeper of order, even if Carolina just wanted to keep peace and order at the dinner table.

Carolina Pennsbury surveyed the group around the circular dining table with thoughtful eyes. She was thinking how hard it is to arrange a stable and satisfied dining group in a retirement home. Someone is always going away for months to rehab or to permanent assisted care or to that place where cares are forever gone, as well as your dining companion. Not to mention the changing that happens when the Snowbirds go to Florida for the winter. Then Management will fill the space if you can't entice an acceptable person from another table, and then the trouble starts again. One or more of your own acceptable, but now dissatisfied, dining companions may be enticed away to another table and you have to decide where your allegiances lie. To move, or not to move, that is the question.

Navigating the dining room can be the hardest work one has to do in the old folks home. Who would have thought? Social skills, luck and good looks are primary to survival in these places, worse than in high school. Don't forget good clothes too. Of course, one would think sentient rationality might be one of the biggest assets one can have here. (If you want to eat while contributing to something resembling the scintillating conversation of the Algonquin Round Table of the 1920s, die younger. Ironically, Harpo Marx, the silent Marx brother in the movies, was often a brilliant member of that Table at one time.) To be honest, a little harmless forgetting might be a bigger asset to combatting the everpresent state of boredom and lack of occupation there, except for the planned activities and "entertainment" that makes completing a jigsaw puzzle the equivalent of being presented with a Nobel Prize by George Clooney.

Carolina thought, *why am I worried? Let the good times roll as long as they can.* But she was worried anyway. It was something Annie had said to her the other day; "Something is wrong here." Yes, something is wrong here. But this is no detective novel using that plot device (never done better than by Dame Agatha). Annie had really said there was something wrong, and she was usually shrewd about people and as practical as a can opener. Was she talking about the place or our group? Was it a general impression or something in particular?

Carolina looked around the room and then at the people at the table. She thought, *there are some normal, balanced people in this place, but not at our table.* They do have peculiarities—at our ages everyone had at least one refined one, or else we were brain dead. Our table refined theirs to the finest grade of ore imaginable. *Except for me, of course*, thought Carolina.

Next to Carolina was her close friend Annie, a woman who carried herself like a soldier but who was kind to those with good intentions. People liked her. She was not the leader of the pack but could fight off a mean act with a comment warning the offending dog not to mess with her. And there were always those trying to be top dog or to increase their place in the pecking order. From the dog packs of high school to the hen houses of the old folks home, it never stopped. Annie had this way of telling you something she saw that others might not have seen. But she forgot it if you were not with her soon enough so she could tell you, or if other things were happening at the same time. She often remembered later. It was her only sign of forgetting, yet. A solid woman of 89 was Annie with children and grandchildren she was proud of. She was happy but asked plaintively from time to time when she was going home—home representing the happiest and most productive time that they all missed. She could be wrong about something she saw too, if a long time had passed since she had seen it. Carolina wondered if there was a way to get her to remember what was bothering her and hoped Annie didn't tell the wrong person.

Dot, an unmarried retired teacher, sat next to Annie. She was wearing a flapper hat from the 1920s. Dot spent her days buying lots of hats on eBay—that is, hats in lots. Her apartment was filled with vintage hats in every room. She sometimes bought strange head forms to put them on from eBay too—some of them with big eyes or grotesque faces painted on them. Some people were actually afraid to go to Dot's apartment— afraid of falling with their canes and walkers and afraid of something sinister in the half-light. They felt like the heads were haunted or that Dot might be a suppressed Lizzie Borden. At least one person had been known to run out of Dot's apartment holding her head and shouting, "They're coming to get me!" Dot looked to be in fine fiddle today, if anyone in these places can be described that way. Carolina thought Dot's hobby was eccentric but amusing. The hats she wore were fun to see.

Lillian was next to Dot with her back against the pillar. She was a tiny woman in her 90s. She had lived very well, you could tell, since she wore designer clothes and commented on every course of food served, describing things they had left out of the recipes with fancy foreign names, probably the expensive things. The residents were served four course meals every night cooked by the worst "chefs," as they were called, and served by the worst servers in the world. (Once in a while the diners heard, hopefully, that one of the cooks had plans of going to chef school someday.) Every day everyone braced themselves for the words they knew were to come from Lillian in her New York Bronx accent by way of Long Island: "How can they serve this? This is NOT food. I know French Onion Soup and it does NOT have American cheese in it. And what kind of bread is there in this soup? Does that look like French bread to you?" Carolina happened to like the way Lillian scrunched up her face in disgust and analyzed what was wrong with the food. She was always right. But her life seemed fixated on the food, which was better not analyzed or discussed. Her dentist son, his wife and her granddaughter visited a lot. She went home with them for weekends. New people at this table usually adjusted to Lillian after a week, or migrated to another table when a place became available. In fact, Lillian had been a relatively recent addition to the circle after a bust-up with a man at another table who just couldn't take "This is NOT food!" one more day. Lillian walked slowly and was one of those quiet dozers in the "library" where it was OK to sleep sitting up but forbidden to do so lying on the couches. Unless the chefs served their (ha ha!) Duck a l'Orange made with chicken and Lillian attacked the chef, Carolina thought she was pretty harmless.

Rita, sitting on the other side of Lillian, seemed quite ordinary, except for one quirk that she had recently acquired. Rita was a lifetime shopper of the first class. Tall, and dark haired even in age, she had perfectly manicured nails. She used to make trips to Europe to buy her clothes. Now Rita too shopped online but for more than hats and heads. (Carolina was thinking that most of the people here weren't online except for the men and some women at their table. Maybe some were getting those online obsessions. Was that the answer to something being wrong?) Luckily, Rita could afford to shop so that was OK. Her dead husband had done very well in business. Her children weren't asking for money—they had plenty and didn't care what their mother did with hers. Most of the residents watched TV and some read in their spare time, and most of their time was spare. Rita's only current problem seemed to be that she had seen a *Hoarders* TV episode in someone's apartment and suddenly was afraid she was a hoarder. She now threw out at least as much as she shopped. Her place was getting sparser every day. Carolina had been deputized to talk to her when someone had found large boxes of stuff in the trash room with Rita's name still in some places on the boxes, although she had tried to remove them all. She swore that she was finished shopping, but more boxes appeared in the trash room while her apartment was becoming bare. When talked to about it, Rita said it was plain to everybody that she had to shop to fill up the empty places in her apartment and drawers. So her drawers were almost empty too. She took to putting boxes in the trash rooms on different floors at night so people wouldn't know they were hers. (Carolina hoped at least the workers here were getting some good out of the situation.) Rita's problem didn't seem very serious if she had as much money as people thought. The condition might even pass if she forgot about that unfortunate program. The warning was out to change the channel when Rita came knocking.

Between Rita and Carolina sat Margie. Carolina thought, "Whatever are we going to do with Margie?" Now Margie was the newest addition to the table and was a problem. Margie was a train wreck, already eaten up and spit out by another table on the other side of the room. She had migrated pathetically around the room until she had floated up as a piece of debris to a vacated chair at this table. Margie was a short, heavy woman in cheap clothes, always dressed in pants that didn't fit. She wore only polyester, reason enough to be rejected by some tables. She looked bedraggled in her wig that revealed her balding head in the back, thick glasses and the same worn out Birkenstock sandals. She was obviously depressed. She had told her dining companions (again and again) that her husband of 25 years had just left her three months ago to chase women on the internet—and then in the flesh. On top of all of this, Margie was disabled with an illness that made her dizzy, which explained her strange footwear choice in a place that expected one to dress up a bit for dinner. She was younger than the rest by 20 years at least. Many residents had children Margie's age. Most of the renters were in their 80s before they came to retirement places with their walkers and memory problems, or their children had made them come. Margie's son had just graduated from college and was doing internships in other States. She had no place else to go—and had signed a year's lease here at $50,000/year. She was stuck, as Management intended to keep her as long as she tottered around and paid up. (This was one of those "for profit" retirement homes.) The group at the current table had seen her evicted from another table where one of the "ladies" had taken an instant dislike to her. Margie later told her new group she never knew why. When she was still assigned to the other table, they would watch (the whole room would watch) as she came into the dining room night after night looking more wilted and shaken every time. No one knew how long she could continue with her misery. They all expected her to break down any night or for Rolanda, the "lady" looking daggers at her, to jump over the table at her. Rolanda, a retired teacher, was accepted as one of the stable, dignified people there. Margie told her new friends that the Dining Room Manager had come to her apartment and had given her the news that she was not wanted at that table and should "try" various other tables to make lots of friends. Eventually she made it to the table in the corner— the one that accepted eccentricities. Everyone supposed Management was watching with their fingers crossed.

Now, on the positive side, Margie was well educated, intelligent, had a wry sense of humor and could retrieve walkers at the end of a meal. If she didn't talk about her husband abandoning her, she was considered a possible asset to the table— AND if she didn't just fall apart, OR say the outrageous things she said about the end of the world according to string theory, OR wander around the place inside and out at all hours looking for a quieter apartment to move to, OR talk like a person who had lived through the sexual revolution of the 1960s in her youth. The women here were single ladies or women who had been married for over 60 years, before being widowed and were accustomed to proper behavior. If one said something "sucked," the conversation stopped and people stared with disapproval at the offender. And they didn't want to hear about those internet sites frequented by that objectionable husband of hers. To do her justice, Margie was a quick learner and tried to be proper, as she saw the others defined it here. She didn't look like a flower child, more like a bag lady, but she was sweet, kind, and terrified. And so fragile. She had potential, but no one was here to do therapy. Too bad the dinners were two hours long and they sometimes had to wait a half hour to be served anything—while they looked at each other. (Where was Harpo Marx when you needed him?) It was hard for people to see this large mass of pain that was Margie every night. And this was no place to cheer up.

So these were Carolina's assessments of the people she spent hours a day with. What about Carolina herself?

Carolina had been Director of a university library and its branches with a distinguished academic career. If you can survive academic politics, you can survive anywhere. She could have existed in an ethical way in the Italian court of the Medici's. Her Church was important to her. The members were her support and her family since her sister had died. Members visited her often, and one family had taken her beloved pets into their home. She dressed neatly in rather old-fashioned skirts and blouses of good quality. Her eyeglasses got thicker each year. She was the kind of person who got vintage pins as gifts rather than diamonds. Carolina lived plainly, with furniture she had acquired in antique and thrift stores with a few beautiful family pieces too. Everyone who visited felt her place was comfortably and tastefully furnished. It just made people feel welcome. They didn't notice the stacks of books in neat shelves around her rooms or the pictures of students smiling in their caps and gowns or the fine oak desk that had been her father's with her computer on it. Somehow she never made anyone feel intimidated by her obvious scholarly ways and accomplishments. Lots of the people here had only finished high school, since they were young during that period when girls were supposed to get married early and have children. Carolina was a strong woman who had encouraged young women all of her life. Her mother had named her after two aunts—Caroline and Ina. She was a Yankee through and through, a Pennsylvania Quaker, although her name misled people into thinking she was a Southern Belle. It was like seeing Katherine Hepburn playing Scarlett O'Hara. Her name caused confusion about her, but she cherished it as a gift from her beloved mother. She had never married. The few men she could have married were taken, and people did keep their vows in those days. At least the men she would have wanted did or she wouldn't have wanted them. People respected Carolina and with reason. She had great compassion for them. She meditated on the admonition of Plato to "Be kind, for everyone you meet is fighting a hard battle." She felt sympathy, especially for those who had lost their places in life, their old lives having dried up with age. Now everyone here was impaired in some way, most with few years left. Old people came to this retirement home having to make new lives among these strange people, and some of them were very strange. Carolina's faith kept her going on an even keel. She prayed that her mind wouldn't go first. Holier than thou? No, though she often thought we all fall short of the glory of God and participate in some way in the seven deadly sins. Not that she was a preachy person, these were just her thoughts when she was alone with her books and the remains of her much loved home by the university. Because of a sight problem, she could no longer drive, although she hid it from the residents here very well. There was no self-pity in Carolina. Her reading aids were inconspicuous, and she read the menu before going down to dinner every night. It was going to be more noticeable someday but she hoped not too soon. Kind friends had found her this place near them where she could visit them and her animal companions that she missed so much. (She just couldn't decide on which one to bring, and she felt they were better off together in that wonderful home with all that space. She had waited to see if one would pine away for her, to know to take that one, but they had all adjusted happily it seemed. They knew she loved them and they were together in spirit.) She had a peaceful spirit, although now she was disturbed by wondering if anyone was breaking one of those seven deadly sins in a big way that would hurt other people. If so, she was going to prevent it if it killed her.

Carolina was jolted out of her reverie by being asked how she was.

Much of the talk in these places was about health and trips to the hospital or other people's trips to the emergency room. Carolina almost said, "Let me suggest something else before we start talking about that again." Knowing her group, she changed it to the easiest thing there was to say, "What do you think about the menu?"

Rita piped up, "It's Wednesday. We get wine on Wednesdays. Remember to ask for it or we won't get it."

Most had forgotten about it. They only remembered when they saw another table getting it and then it was hard to get the server to come over, and most of them "forgot" too. The servers didn't seem to like to serve it, and probably the food manager didn't push it either. Carolina wondered what the alcohol did to all of those prescriptions in their bodies that everyone was taking.

Lillian, commenting on the menu said, "Huh! Look at that. 'Turkey Scaloppini' What's that? They call anything scaloppini. There's nothing on this menu I want. I heard the new food service manager (different from the dining room manager) is going to get rid of the blintzes. What are we going to eat if they take that off the permanent menu? They are just going to add the words 'scaloppini' or 'primavera' to everything. We'll starve."

Annie said, "No, you'll starve. We don't know what is supposed to be in those foreign sounding dishes anyway. What was that *noise* something we had the other night?"

"You mean *Nicoise*"? Lillian scrunched up her face and said, "They just call them fancy names to try to fool us. But they can't fool me."

Dot said, "Remember that night they tried to give us Frito Pie or Bratwurst with Tater Tots? The chef must have been sick that day and they bought the food at some deli. And did you see the man they let in today? He asked someone to cut his food up at breakfast. This is supposed to be independent care. He isn't allowed to have his aide in the dining room, but he can't be asking people to do things like that for him either."

The rest of the table laughed at the thought that only people who were independent lived here. Of course "Independent Care" meant different things to different retirement homes. Here it seemed to be what the other residents would bear. Here there were people in their rooms all of the time who didn't bother anyone because they couldn't get up without help, but who had full time aides. No one cared, or almost no one. There are always people who object to anything crossing a line because they can't stand anyone breaking rules or who do it or for petty motives. (Petty motives can be a good reason for revenge.) Some places force you into their more expensive assisted care or even their nursing home, an action the resident usually dreads. Those places can be grim with no privacy. But here there was no assisted care, so the place would have to lose a resident. Some places even require a cognitive test before they let a person in, so they aren't stuck with residents who eventually can't pay and will need lots of care later. Those places usually required large buy-ins of hundreds of thousands of dollars first. Here you don't pay your rent, you're out. Senior care is so complicated in rules as well as interpretation: senior homes and apartments, independent care, assisted care, rehab, nursing homes. Choices abound and are not always voluntary, but one's comfort and happiness depends on making the right ones.

Dot added, "Driving makes a difference. You are sort of normal anywhere if you can drive where you want. Blanche told me her children stole her license plate from her car to make her quit driving. It was that last accident she said."

Carolina thought there are even some residents who have cars and friends and sometimes a part time job who choose to live here. Most people would die to be able to drive and live really independently if they could again. I would. The ones who seem really independent must have secrets they are hiding. But you never know about people. Aloud, she said, "One couple told me they are here because the wife simply refuses to cook anymore. She must have been a really bad cook to come here."

Everyone nodded and laughed.

They ate for a while in silence. All of them were tired and quiet by the time the entrées came and were certified as right by the diners. Everyone had had to wait until the whole table had shown up before they could order and wait for the soup and wait for the salad and wait for their various entrees with the right vegetables.

That night the silence was broken when a not unusual sound came over from the table behind them that carried through to their side of the dining room: "You're nobody 'til somebody loves you…." Rita, whose hearing was still good, said, "Oh, it's Milton again."

CHAPTER TWO—VIEW OF ANOTHER TABLE

Milton was a man seated behind their table who would suddenly burst out in song from time to time. He also told jokes, mostly of a slightly risqué bent. He could have gone on the stage as a song and gag man, at least in the Catskills. He was in his 90s and knew all of the old songs and all of the old jokes.

"That should NOT be allowed," Dot said of his singing.

Carolina said, "I sort of enjoy it. I ate over there the other day when most of you weren't here and his mind is remarkable for 93. He knows the words to every old song I could think of. And jokes. He asked me to mention a subject, any subject, and I said Chet Huntley, that TV newscaster from the black and white TV era, and he had a joke ready. How many people do you know who can do that?"

"I like him too. Tell us the joke," Annie said.

"Chet Huntley fell in love with a pota…"

Carolina was interrupted by people yelling at Milton to stop singing. Not everyone appreciated Milton. In fact, there was one man who had almost come to blows with Milton when he burst out in exuberant song in the so-called library and disturbed the only resident who insisted the library was only for reading. That very person was one of those shouting to Milton to shut up. Milton ignored them and their dirty looks. He didn't care. He shut up only because his next course had come. Milton liked to eat.

Seated with Milton was his wife, Maxine, who also was often annoyed with Milton, but once was seen by Carolina kissing Milton in the elevator as the door closed when she was about to get on. Nobody ever believed Carolina about that although she never lied.

A very thin woman sat next to Maxine. Beverly was very, very thin with very, very good clothes and a very, very wrinkled face with lots and lots of heavy make-up. How many women at 94 wore the highest of high heels on the home's bus and refused help getting on with heavy packages because she claimed she was like a teenager—a teenager. She had very, very thick jet black hair in a bouffant curly do. People wondered if it was hers, although she never said. She was usually loud but polite to people, although Margie said that when she had told Beverly that she had to wear Birkenstock shoes and couldn't wear heels, Beverly pointed to her own very high heels and said, "That's because you have let yourself go." Hurt, Margie took her rotund body out of there and got on the bus. Beverly was known for skipping meals to maintain her too slight frame if she ate over five calories extra for breakfast, and announced to everyone she met that she never ate lunch. She was the sort who would get plastic surgery; maybe she had done her utmost but she still looked old, although she dressed like a fashionable socialite in her twenties—but from the 1950s.

Now for Ike, who also sat at that table. Everyone felt Ike's personal power. Ike didn't care what anyone thought about him. Even Carolina, the wise and calm, fell under his spell. But it was Margie who had the best description of Ike in one line: The head of a lion and the morals of a gangster. Ike gave the impression that the only thing he was religious about was poker which he played every day—a group of the men did. (Women were NOT welcome and had to organize their own table when there were enough who wanted to play, but women stuck mostly to bridge.) Ike was blunt. Margie was thrilled one day when she met him in the elevator and was telling him about how she had paid over $2,000 for activity fees to get into the Buckingham Courte while everyone laughed at her, many had even gotten incentives to come, probably partly paid for by her. Ike told her to suck it up and quit complaining. Margie's heart beat fast from admiration.

Ike had a steady girlfriend, Alma, in a nearby retirement home who visited often or he drove there. Both had grown children which made marriage difficult, although everyone knew Ike could do whatever he wanted. Alma was sweet and had been elegant. Sometimes she moved to music she heard and you could see how graceful and fun she had been. Some people were catty and would introduce them as Mr. and Mrs., making it necessary for Ike or Alma to correct them. Alma's health and mind had recently been fading, making the cruises they often took together in winter not always possible now. It seemed to the others that the woman was more attached to the gentleman than he was to her, from remarks he sometimes made about other women, but no one really knew.

Two vacant chairs were left at that table for any leftovers for Management to fill if there was an extra diner or two floating around. The seating varied somewhat from night to night with floaters from other tables, as new people came in or others ate with their families at another table or a few ate in their apartments if they were ill. (At a charge for delivery, of course.) The diners from tables with few numbers on any given night were redistributed, an occurrence most dreaded since old people hate change and are unsure of their welcome at a new table even if temporary.

Margie and Carolina had talked about Ike when they were alone one day. "Alpha male" said Carolina. Margie said "He is Hot! I find it hard not to tell him so in case he doesn't know it. I love tall, selfish men, I guess. Look whom I married. Anyway, I can see him running a sweat shop and calling girls "honey" and firing them for not having sex with him. I mean it is his birthright. He won medals in the war too, you know."

One day a group of women consolidated from other tables happened to be seated without men at Maxine's table for dinner.

Lillian (probably jealous, thought Carolina) said it was not right for a nice Jewish girl like Alma to live in sin like she did.

"So what? It is their business," Maxine said

"What does he see in her? She does not even dress well," said Rita, also out of jealousy probably.

Maxine said, "If Ike doesn't care about how she dresses, why should we?" But inside she thought, *girl?* Alma was 90 if she was a day.

"He probably isn't even faithful," added Dot.

"Ike is handsome with his white curly hair, and brilliant, and rich. I heard him talking about millions he gave away. He is like a tycoon among us," Margie said.

Betty, an outspoken woman who used to eat at Carolina's table before she went to rehab and was replaced by Management with Lillian, closed the conversation down when she said, "So Ike is a goy and a schmuck, so what?"

No other man had this effect on the women in this old folks home. Maybe Floyd, but he was more slick than hot.

CHAPTER THREE—MARCH OF THE
WALKER BRIGADE

The server came to Carolina's table with the desserts. All of the regulars were there, and everyone had ordered a dessert.

Margie commented, "It isn't fair that the choice is between New York cheesecake or fruit or one of those sugar-free cookies. Some people eat that fruit every night and they are not even thin!" She repeated, "Not fair," as she ate her cheesecake, some at the table would say gobbled as she did all of her food. Annie was always suggesting in a concerned tone that she eat more slowly.

They all agreed about the unfairness of dessert because it was true, although Lillian still looked with disapproval on "fat people" eating dessert. The group never got coffee with their dessert. For some reason they got dessert and then later were asked what they wanted to drink. They often got coffee or tea just before the Dining Room Manager sent someone around to collect their tablecloth because the second seating diners were waiting for the table. The diners stood their ground for a few minutes on such occasions but prepared to leave, knowing like Captain Piccard that all resistance was futile.

Leaving the dining room—now that was a story to be told by Kafka or maybe one of the great dreary Russian writers like Gogol or just Alfred Hitchcock. Carolina thought of it as the procession of the walkers.

Margie collected the walkers parked along the walls for Annie, Dot, and Lillian. Rita used a cane which she had leaned against the wall or the pillar within reaching distance, but she could still get around well and use steps. Carolina had a cane too she rarely used. Being in the back made leaving the long dining room a problem. The room consisted of tables of different sizes staggered a bit so there was only a small central lane in and out where two walkers side by side wouldn't fit. People leaving without an appliance had to wait for people in walkers sandwiched between them—all dodging the servers setting up for the next seating. All movement stopped when a wheel chair needed the whole space to maneuver. Those exiting also had to take into consideration people talking to those still seated. Annie was one of those, nodding majestically like a queen to those seated and talking graciously to them. (This behavior made the Dining Room Manager turn magenta.) It was good for many that she was let go when the new food service came in. Some of the diners hated her for yelling across the dining room, telling them to leave, she needed the table. The selected diners she did this to grumbled that they had not gotten their coffee. That is when the table cloth removal tactic had begun. The manager didn't care if they had just been served coffee—they and the tablecloth had to go.

Then the walker brigade filing out was held up by an elbow in the line where they had to make a left turn into a hall and right turn soon after. (One could tell this place was designed with great thought.) By then, there were two lines with diners coming and going—and stopping to talk to each other going in different directions. "What should I order?" etc. By that time most of those leaving couldn't remember what had been on the menu. And there were calls from the people behind them to "move along." Woe to the impatient person trying to bypass the line by passing in the middle. It took a person with a mean disposition (mostly a man) to brave the dirty looks and remarks of the people who were obeying the traffic conventions. Not to mention there was really no room to move down the middle, and one might topple over one of the frail people in their walkers. Every night. Navigating the halls and elevators was not easy in busy times like between dinner seatings.

The building was one of those common to retirement homes, made up of two or three long wings of three or four floors each with a library/reception room on the first floor across from a majestic wooden concierge desk as one came in the central entrance. This particular building had four floors and two long wings connected by a shorter wing with apartments running parallel on each side of the corridors. There was an elevator on each end of the building and exits outside of those wings as well as a central elevator and exit in the wing connecting them. With fobs (name used for keys), residents could enter pretty much anonymously and anyone at all could leave that way too, especially during quiet hours. It was not difficult to enter the building using the main entrance either, the concierge was often in the back office or helping someone or setting up the video room for a movie or something. Motion detectors were everywhere but no cameras, although there were rumors there were hidden cameras. The rumors were spread by the workers, maybe to keep the residents in line. Maybe there were cameras. But residents doubted that Management would buy anything they didn't have to by law.

The dining hours were the busiest in the entrance area. Residents stopped to get their mail in boxes inconveniently placed across from the main elevator and around the corner from the concierge desk. The wheel chairs and walkers came to a dead stop with people waiting for the elevator to come down, while people using the elevator held it up on other floors to wait for the people with walkers or wheel chairs to get off or just to finish their conversations. The wisest and nimblest of the former diners who wanted to get to their apartments used the side elevators or visited in the library to talk to the second seaters waiting for the dining room to be navigable. There were boxes behind the concierge desk too where they got their newspapers that were held in much needed protective custody for them and where they got their bills and notices from the Management. There was a line for this service too after dinner, and there were more people to navigate around in the lobby, like residents meeting their relations to take in to dinner or be taken out.

Then evening activities, such as they were, began.

CHAPTER FOUR—EVENING MEETINGS AND DOINGS

Annie, being a sociable person, loved the library after dinner. She especially loved getting out of the dining room early to hear old songs being played on the piano by resident Floyd in the video/entertainment room next to the library. Ike, as mentioned before, was HOT but Floyd was slick, slick, slick. He too was in his 90s but you wouldn't know it. Margie didn't and still couldn't believe it when told. (Annie had gotten Margie to go with her to these "concerts" when available or to join her after dinner, since sometimes the second seaters formed a circle and were not welcoming to outsiders. Annie and Margie would sit alone and talk until joined by people who were finished with dinner or until it was time for the movie, although Margie balked at going to the movie since she had seen most of them on TCM recently.)

Getting back to Floyd. Floyd wore sports shirts open at the top and slacks and polished snakeskin shoes. He was always surrounded by at least ten women (Margie counted them) and tried to play his way into their hearts (and beds, some people thought). He loved women and women seemed to love him. He did love music too, his apartment sounded of classical music most of the time, even as he played his cello along with recorded music. Music and women were Floyd's passions. He was in a good place for women's attention, although he was one of the snowbirds who disappeared to Florida every year as women wept for his loss. (He must have known the pleasure of what it was like to have been at your own funeral many times.) It may just have been that Hialeah was calling but that was speculation. Carolina was safe from Floyd's charms and thought he reminded her of "Georgie Porgie." You remember, he kissed the girls and made them cry but when the boys came out to play…. The other men didn't SEEM jealous.

Usually the group from the back table made their way out into the lobby where Annie got her paper from the concierge and put it in her walker for later, Margie was often with her, Lillian joined the people in the library, while others made their separate ways upstairs. When Floyd was playing the piano, Annie and Margie always went to the entertainment room. Floyd played until the second shift of diners entered the dining room and often a little after, if he was getting enough appreciation.

About six people were there one night—Ike and his girlfriend and her daughter having come in too. Some of those present actually sang, most having forgotten the words. Each remembered the songs that had been important to them for special reasons. Margie, born after World War II, surprisingly, knew them all but had no voice for singing.

This was one of Margie's lucky days. Being near Ike excited her, and his girlfriend was busy talking to her daughter who had driven her over. Floyd played until the second seating was gone to the dining room and ended with "All of Me." Suddenly, Ike turned to Annie and, over Margie's head, said, "Will you take all of me, Annie?" Annie laughed. She wasn't that impressed by Ike for some reason, but she did seem to be liked by most men. She was a friendly person. Margie felt a pang of jealously. She was 25 or more years younger than most people here, but knew that men liked thin and elegant, walkers or age didn't matter. Maybe really young and thin and hot would matter but not just younger if also fat. Then Floyd said he had to leave for dinner but would play someone a special song, "Once in a While." Ike muttered, "That's the story of my life, once in a while." Only Margie seemed to hear and wondered what the relationship was like between Ike and Alma. It was odd that a man like Ike should have such a problem, if he truly did. Margie just wanted him to notice her like most of the women did.

They all filed out of the room with Annie and Margie going to their rooms. Annie would go down alone for the movie later, hoping for company, although sometimes she was the only person in the video room. In the elevator, Margie thought, *Maybe I should wear my red wig sometime.*

Annie and Margie got out of the elevator on the same floor. Margie was still living in the second floor model apartment with the model furniture, since she had moved so hurriedly from her joint condo that she hadn't picked out an apartment of her own. She had never seen this place before she had become a resident of it. She had her furniture on hold with the moving people for a month now and counting. She HAD to find an apartment soon. She had an obsession with quiet. She needed to hear no banging or beeping. Her nerves were worn. Nobody understood that here the workers didn't care about noise since they had to be awake, and the other residents were half deaf or had the quiet places. Margie's hearing was acute, hearing things most of the others didn't. So Margie wandered the halls day and night looking for an available apartment that was quiet. The ones they showed her all seemed to be over the air conditioners outside or near elevators that dinged especially loudly for the near deaf or were across from trash rooms with clanging doors where people dropped their bags through the heavy metal door of the trash chute to the compactor below. She found that empty apartments were usually unlocked so she wandered into them to sit on the couches in the model apartments or on the floor in the empty ones to listen for sounds in the dark. So people saw her looking bedraggled in her wanderings day and night, sometimes in the middle of the night, since she had insomnia. She wandered outside too on the sidewalks around the big building, looking for things that might make sounds under the apartments, like the kitchen or fans or dumpsters or neighboring tennis courts. There was always something. She was frantic to find a suitable apartment. Management was giving her a deadline and she was tired of people pointedly asking, "Did you find an apartment yet, Margie?" She herself was disgruntled, since she had picked out two apartments she would have accepted, but found repairs that she herself had discovered needed to be made in each one of them on her vigils in them. But then Management said it wasn't worth it to them to fix them and she had to pick out another apartment that was empty. So she wandered and got more bedraggled and a reputation as odd. She would sometimes sing songs softly or hum them to express her overwhelming feelings, thinking she was alone, but she sometimes wasn't. People did not want someone in their "neighborhood" walking with her head down singing things like "How Can I Live Without You?" or more often, "Your Cheatin' Heart" or "You Can't Hide Your Lyin' Eyes." Being in the middle of a divorce that she didn't want, didn't help her nerves either. Thank heavens people like Annie and Carolina understood and accepted her. But she was a mess and she knew it. And she saw quite a few things she didn't understand on her expeditions around the old folks homestead. Things she told Annie about on those nights she felt well enough to make it to Annie's room in the evening to keep her company.

Margie thought she could see things going on within these empty hallways and unwatched entrances— workers, families, strangers, all of whom the residents had learned to ignore. She would feel uneasy when out of the corner of her eye she would see an unexpected shadow or feel a presence. Being in a home for seniors, she knew that not a few of the apartments she had looked at and stayed in alone for a few hours had been visited by the Grim Reaper. Ordinarily, this did not bother her, but sometimes when she saw a shadow that seemed to move or heard noises of people talking in an empty place, she shivered. She didn't know if the fear she felt was for something alive or dead.

Annie did not know what to think, but listened as a comfort to Margie and to have company herself.

CHAPTER FIVE—CAROLINA TAKES HER WALK

Instead of making that second turn out of the dining room with her dining companions, Carolina made her way straight down the hall to get to the elevator on her side of the building. She passed the darkened beauty parlor and employees' lounge and some mechanical rooms, as well as some residents shuffling along in their walkers to dinner and exchanged greetings. "Don't order the trout and brownies," was her advice on dinner. She came to the elevator and had to decide whether to go on to her outdoors walk from the exit a little farther along or go to her room. She decided to take her walk indoors later that night and went to the 4th floor. She got out of the elevator, surprised again at how dim and empty the halls were. Most of the end apartments on most floors were empty. She had heard that Management had given orders to fill them. There were lots of recent financial "incentives" to new people, while the longtime residents paid their higher rents with the yearly increases added on. There were some hard feelings on the part of the older residents who felt they were carrying the new peoples' lower rates.

Carolina opened her door to see a generic senior apartment but furnished with comfort. In it, were gifts from around the world she had received from friends on their sabbaticals and vacations, some quite valuable she thought, but she kept things her heart valued—rich or inexpensive. She was sure other people had valuable things in their rooms too.

The windows were on one side of the room only, since the other walls were attached to other apartments or lined the corridors. The windows on that one side were enormous, going from ceiling to near the floor. She loved looking out at night at the timbered neighborhood. The sunsets on her side of the building were magnificent.

Carolina took her medications and sat at her desk facing the windows to work on a paper on Thomas Hardy. She thought what a change it was not to sit facing the door to see whatever people were coming to her office. It was refreshing to have time with no interruptions or distractions. But she couldn't concentrate on the character of Sue Bridehead in *Jude the Obscure* whom she saw as a more obnoxious character than did the usual critic. Everyone saw her through Jude's eyes, who had the worst judgments of women. Or they saw her as new feminist. Carolina saw the carnage surrounding Sue from her first lover to her husband to Jude, some of it to body and some to soul, and thought differently. She wished she could call her article "Sue Bridehead as Medusa." Or maybe she should work on the meaning of Arabella, Jude's wife, who seemed to bump improbably into some of the characters at the end of the book and have unlikely conversations with them that spurred the plot on to a quicker, deadly finish. But Carolina couldn't concentrate on her scholarly work this evening.

She thought of her three cats and one dog lying by the big fireplace tonight with the big garden to run in and that dear family to love them. Did any of them miss her as much as she missed them? Had she made the right decisions for them all?

And what was going on here? She had felt that something was wrong herself before Annie had said anything. Maybe Margie, with all of her drama and being out of place, had disturbed their spirits. Margie had so many conflicts. If one thought about it, there were many motives for doing away with people here and many people to do away with—if the feeling was about violence and not just grand or petty theft. Mere money laundering would be just fine with her.

Margie had talked about all of those unlocked apartments that looked like someone had been in them from time to time. She said some of them would suddenly be locked and then unlocked again a few hours later, even on Sundays when neither repair staff nor marketers were on the premises. Carolina herself had seen a janitor coming out of one with what looked like a pile of folded laundry. He looked startled when she saw him, and she wondered if he was just doing his laundry in an empty apartment or if something else was in the basket.

Some residents kept saying they missed things like one emerald earring and had even called the police. Some found their missing things in strange places in their apartments where they probably had left them, and some by-standers suspected that family members might be keeping the more expensive items "safe." Nobody believed the old residents who did have memory problems in general. Carolina thought there might be something to it. But then there were the people who thought people were stealing their kitchen sponges or replacing their detergent with another brand.

Aides and cleaners and marketing people came and went everywhere. Everyone knew by experience that there was a double set of keys off the concierge desk to use when people got locked out of their apartments by accident. Anyone at all could get those keys by sneaking in there when the concierge was distracted.

Then there were the arguments. Margie was either liked very much or disliked a lot. Was she as meek as she seemed? She was troubled, poor thing. There were the usual arguments between people about nothing from time to time too. Carolina remembered the time a woman was stopped from putting out too many Chanukah decorations, since Management claimed they would have had to put out more Christmas decorations to balance them. No one found out who had complained to the Management. Or maybe someone had.

Then there was the time Rolanda had tried to have current dogs banned from all public areas except the halls where they would leave to go out for their walks, and she wanted to have all future ones totally banned from occupancy. (Betty's Rusty had disrupted a singer during a Friday program.) About three residents with dogs showed up to plan a protest with Betty and Rusty, but Management let it be known they would never deprive a resident of their (approved) companion (or lose a possible resident who might have a dog). All dogs would have to be leashed when outside of their apartments (even the small, cute ones). Betty said someone had known Rolanda before she came here and could tell us stories about her troublemaking. Carolina admitted there were still hard feelings about the dog feud. Lots of people had taken sides.

Could poker or bridge losses be the "something wrong" here? Carolina didn't think they played for much, if anything.

What about that smell like herbs being smoked in the halls of those empty apartments? Was it simple pot smoking by bored workers in the vacant apartments or a bigger drug operation?

Would anyone get violent over the dining room machinations? The Dining Room Manger was detested by some, but she received orders every day from MANAGEMENT who were in another State, some said another country. All of the Management here got orders at a meeting every morning. They were all puppets, but some were kind and some meaner than others in how they carried out their orders.

That's enough, Carolina thought. *I think I'll take that walk now. Where's that cane? It's dark in some of those halls.* She felt her cane for heft. *I could do some damage with this.*

She left her apartment. Residents were home for the night or at the movie and a few were out with family. Most were home. She walked down the long hall to the cross wing and over to the next wing. Some people had generic wreaths on their doors as well as their names and a few had figurines by their door in the corner. (A good place to hide things?) She heard TVs and dishes and music and voices from the apartments. She heard one "ideal" couple berating each other. How surprising, at least to Carolina. You never know about people. There were lots of empty apartments at the end of this wing, with a convenient fire exit so one wouldn't have to take the elevator if one could do steps. She tried one of the empty apartment doors and it opened. She went in it to find furniture and kitchen belongings left over from people who had left, and heard a toilet running. Maybe the dirty apartment was open to make it easier for various repair people to get in and out. She didn't see anything suspicious and left. She noticed that Rolanda's apartment was here across from the exit. She hoped Margie wasn't looking at the empty apartment next to it. Carolina would have to mention something to warn Margie about that.

As she turned, she saw Margie coming down the long hall towards her. For once, Margie smiled without that look of desperation about it. Margie laughed and immediately began pouring out a story. "I was looking at one of those apartments I might rent and came out to bump into Joyce, you know, the dignified lady at the table beside us on the other side of the wall. I was telling her about my husband who left me after 25 years to chase women, and she just said loudly, "'That son of a bitch!' That's all she said. She made me feel so good."

Carolina smiled for her but counseled, "Margie, be careful about walking the halls at night. I just don't think it's good to be alone out here too late."

"But I have to find an apartment," was Margie's only response. She couldn't understand not only that there was not perfect security here or anywhere, but that she'd get a bad reputation among people for wandering and that wasn't good if she wished to live here. Margie had actually accidentally opened an unlocked occupied apartment one time to the anger of a resident who didn't appreciate it.

Carolina said "good night" and watched as fat little Margie wandered away quickly down the fire exit stairs towards her own room, hopefully. Carolina listened until Margie got safely to another floor. Margie was singing "I Will Survive..." Now that seemed to show an improvement in her state of mind. But ditzy confusion seemed to be her Karma, as some people would say. Most people couldn't figure out if she was an airhead or extremely intelligent. Carolina herself wished healing for her and for her to find a home.

Carolina took the elevator to another floor and continued her "walk" without meeting anyone else. She passed an apartment and saw a key token attached to the wreath on the door—the people here probably thought it meant come in. But for whom? She passed the model apartment Margie was still in and it was quiet. She hoped Margie was finally going to bed. She passed Annie's apartment who must still be at the movies or her TV would be on.

Carolina passed Ike's apartment in another wing. She had to admit she would love to be invited into the environs, which she heard were posh. But what she wanted to be invited in for, even she didn't know. (Carolina did not blame herself for this feeling, it was just the effect Ike had on women.) There was some jealousy over Ike and Floyd. Did some woman want to cut down on the competition? She remembered Margie's and others' looks of jealousy when Ike had said, "Man, look at that figure" when 90+ year old Beverly went by in her high heels. She wondered what her own face had looked like. She was aware that people were supposed to be randy in these old age homes—their drawers were supposed to be filled with Viagra. But surely not here. Except for one or two, and maybe not even those, the old people here acted like they were supposed to, thank heaven. They were not adding to that growing number of elderly people spreading STDs like the internet news proclaimed. Carolina hoped that was all media hype.

She made her way to the first floor at the farthest entrance from her own apartment. She looked from the elevator down the hall to the outside exit. Most residents picked apartments near the main elevator that were closest to the dining and activity rooms because of their mobility problems. The end apartments on the first floor in this area were empty except for one. Why would anyone pick the end one with the sounds of the intercom and door banging and cold from the winter coming in, affecting you, when there were so many other apartments to choose from nearby? Carolina made a note to check to see if the resident was deaf so he didn't care about noise and ask him why he had picked that apartment. The name on the door was a man's. It was certainly a discreet location for letting people in and out of the building. Cars could park in the next lot and would not have to pass by the home's apartments with the big windows and possibly be seen by the residents looking out, if the building were being used as a drop off point for illegal articles.

Carolina saw some residents come in the side door with their fob after eating out. She said hello. An unaccompanied aide came in behind them, which was not right since aides were supposed to come in the main entrance and sign in and out at the concierge desk, but that was a longer walk to the side wings. They all came in the most convenient way when they could.

Carolina made her way by the concierge desk, saw that the library was empty, but some people were in the dark video room. She walked towards the far elevator that would take her up to her apartment. On the way, she saw Floyd walking a woman named Carrie Ann down the first floor hall. Carrie Ann was one of those flighty women who would have worn big fake daisies on her bonnet in another century. Carolina didn't know her well. Second seating. Floyd was singing, "Hey Carrie Ann, what's your game girl, can anybody play?" The song seemed to be dated after Floyd's youth but Floyd was often surprising. Carrie Ann seemed pleased with the company and not needing rescuing. Carolina passed by with a "Hello" and got to the elevator before she saw if Floyd was welcomed into Carrie Ann's apartment or not. She didn't think so.

Before she got back to the elevator, she had passed an apartment with an open door she had never seen inside before. She saw a larger than life size Buddha in front of the giant windows with oriental plants and statues tastefully placed around the living room. It took her breath away. She would look up who lived there in the directory. The apartment had obviously been done by a professional decorator with no expense spared as they say. Why had the door been propped open? Carolina thought there was a lot going on here that she didn't know, and some other people worth meeting. Maybe they passed for those ordinary ones she saw daily?

She thought one can't ignore the possibility that more residents are living longer and have relatives who may be tired of waiting for what is left.

And one can forget that people here may know things they shouldn't about others. We are lonely for the most part and need close friends and confidants. There can't be plotters in the midst to take advantage of the vulnerable people here, still... Carolina thought she would ask around if anyone was writing their memoirs. There must be things people wouldn't want known. But this group was small potatoes—no ex-celebrities or anything like that she knew of. Someone said they once knew Nelson Rockefeller, but there were no actual Rockefellers here.

Carolina got to the door with her name on it. As she looked in her foyer mirror, she thought, "What am I doing? Let's face it, some of the people here are just plain nuts!"

CHAPTER SIX—FIRE ALARM

Carolina settled at her desk for the night, getting an e-mail from her poet friend disagreeing totally with her interpretation of Sue Bridehead. The phone rang. She answered it from her desk and heard nothing. She asked several times if the person on the other end was experiencing difficulty with the line but heard no response and no click. Finally, Carolina hung up. Some child? But it was late.

She got ready for bed, checked the lock on her door and put up the chain. She hoped her friends had done the same. All of the while Carolina was thinking: These halls and trash rooms are really empty most of the time. One is vulnerable here if one thinks about it. But nearly everyone everywhere is physically vulnerable at some time of the day. Still, Margie was probably wandering and trying unlocked apartments with some success and Rita might be carrying her things to the trash. (Carolina wondered if she should check the trash rooms in the morning and get the things back to Rita somehow.)

Sitting up in bed in her cotton nightgown with no Mrs. Santa Claus cap yet, Carolina read *Adam Bede*. Finally, she put her glasses on the night table, turned out the light and fell into a deep sleep.

She opened her eyes in fear to hear the worst fire alarm in the world, much louder than any noise safe for one's ears. It was the equivalent of leaning on a foghorn, worse maybe. It vibrated too, for the deaf and blind one guessed, and bright halogen type lights flashed on and off, for the deaf too? The alarm succeeded in scaring the seniors out of their senses. One had to experience the overpowering effect of it to know what it was like. Carolina put on her clothes from yesterday, got her keys and opened her door. She went back for her ear plugs that she had bought after she had first heard the alarm being tested. She left for the hall, hearing the big fire doors close automatically as they were doing all over the building. She knew the elevators had stopped operating as they were designed to do when the alarm sounded.

She wondered if she should make the climb down all of those levels on the stairs. Her knee was a bit of a problem, but she could hold on to the railing in the dim stairwells. The bright flashing lights even there were blinding and one saw only flashes of what was ahead. They were mentally disorienting, especially the first time one experienced them or if one was groggy with some kind of medication. How easy it would be to make someone fall in this commotion. Of course, she went out like the well trained School Matron she was, still setting an example for her students. She met a few more people as she got near the first floor. She often went to the lobby instead of out the nearest exit door to find out what the problem was, if she didn't actually smell smoke, making sure she could make her way back if necessary (a choice she would scold others about). She did that tonight to see the same people during fire evacuations as usual in the lobby and outside the main entrance. The concierge said the problem was on the 3rd floor but he didn't know what.

He called out to say that they all had to leave the building NOW.

People did not leave their apartments unless they could manage steps or were already on the first floor. There was a list of people staying in their apartments for the fire department to evacuate. Out Carolina went. At least the weather was mild, although some people went to sit in their cars parked around the building. There were some people who were mobile who didn't leave their apartments for fire alarms, even though there were real fires from time to time, like kitchen fires. But mostly these alarms were nothing, so people became complaisant.

Outside, Carolina saw her nearest neighbor, a former dancer who still taught children part time, Ike, Milton, and Maxine, plus a lot of the second seaters. Annie, Lillian and Dot never came down. Carolina said hello to Rita and saw Margie coming from her exit door to join the other people in the center. The fire truck flashed its lights as the firefighters came on the scene. All that flashing gave people headaches, especially people who got migraines. Margie was in her polyester nightgown with a light jacket covering the top but her bottom half showing through against the lights she passed. Ah, Margie. She was very upset, saying to the group that she had only come down to see if there was a real fire. If so, she had to go back for her cat who was hiding in a closet. (It was like Margie to come out to see if she should go back into a burning building.) She said she couldn't catch her cat and put her in the carrier, and Apolonia might run away in panic if she carried her out without it. She wore her baseball cap since she didn't have time to put on her wig to hide her balding head. Didn't she see everyone was dressed in their day clothes or wore a dressing gown over nightclothes? Margie told Carolina that she hoped Rolanda wasn't there. She wasn't. For once something had worked out for Margie.

The alarm stopped and everyone turned to go back. Margie walked outside back toward her own exit and climbed up to her floor to comfort her cat. Most of the others went to the library to wait for the elevators to be turned on. Milton came in to say the firefighters had found the alarm pulled on the 3ʳᵈ floor and there was no reason they could figure out. No fire.

Carolina got into the central elevator with the remaining group who got off on the second and third floors. She was alone going to the 4ᵗʰ floor. Then she had that long walk to her own hall and down it. She walked alone. She had two fire doors to open and two stairwell exits to pass. She remembered that phone call. It was so eerie in these compartments, especially the one that was between two closed fire doors. She wished she had her cane. She was glad her cats and dog were not with her tonight in the apartment during this, although she could only have had one of them. She heard a noise as one of the doors was opened behind her. She suddenly felt a menacing presence. She looked for an occupied apartment to knock on, but there was nobody here who could get to their door quickly enough. She looked for an empty apartment in which to hide. The door of the nearest one was locked. She tried to make it to the door of the next one. It was unlocked but it was too late. She looked back to see who was coming up right behind her.

The concierge said, "How are you after all of that excitement?" He was opening the fire doors so they would stay open.

"Oh, you startled me," she stammered to cover her loss of breath. "It was so quiet here. What do you think triggered the alarm?"

"I have no idea." He held the next fire door open for her and she got to her apartment. She opened her door quickly. It locked behind her.

She sat down in a chair in relief. What a silly woman she was becoming. Maybe next time she would sit in her room until she smelled the smoke too. Probably not. She might go down to breakfast just to see how everyone was in the morning. Then she found herself saying out loud, "Who or what would I have found if I had entered that empty apartment?"

CHAPTER SEVEN—CAROLINA OBSERVES A DAY OF ACTIVITIES

Breakfast. Did she have to go? Carolina thought, *I should go down to sleuth but it is so much easier to make a yolk-free omelet here.* But in the dining room, if you sit with someone who won't leave, the etiquette is you must stay until he or she finishes or someone else sits down. That could take forever. Then there are the glares when someone has taken another's seat. The arguments over this are rare but painful. Poor Margie was bullied off two breakfast tables, one by a man standing by her with a giant cane insisting four times that the table was full (although she was the only person sitting there), each time speaking more loudly until she took all of the dishes and coffee she had laid out in front of her to another table. Mention breakfast and Margie looks like a puppy rescued at the last minute from a professional dogfight. Margie tried taking Danish up to her room from time to time but Management sent a memo to everyone about that practice not being allowed and citing the social aspect of breakfast. (The memo did not mention residents carrying free food up to their aides who seemed to be waiting hungrily for muffins squashed in purses or in the storage compartments of walkers.)

Of course, people were plentiful at breakfast and ready to talk on a one to one basis and more alert than later. She should go, but after that fire alarm business, she just didn't want to. That is what retirement is about, isn't it? Not having to do the things one didn't care to. "Now, Carolina, where is your sense of responsibility and maturity? Discipline, girl." Lack of responsibility won. She decided to go for a little walk and then check her memo box and see if there was anything going on today on the daily activities list. It was Friday, when the residents were supposed to live it up with a glass of wine and entertainment for an hour.

She dressed, took the elevator to her exit and walked around the outside of the building. She entered the main entrance and got her "mail." She saw several people in the library reading their newspapers. There was one provided by the Management with holes cut out of it—no doubt, news items that other residents wanted. The later in the day, the less of the paper; sometimes even sections were gone. No one was ever caught cutting the articles or coupons out. How could that be, when it was out here in the open? (She should know, that happened in libraries all of the time.) Did they take the paper to the nearby bathroom? Maybe the concierges across the way didn't care. But it was considered a most serious offense by people who wanted to read the paper. What was left was kept for a few days and provided a semi-useful reference.

Two women called her over to the newspaper table to talk, but Carolina felt they would be disturbing the man seriously reading the paper. Instead, she said *hello* and sat in an armchair on the side of the fake fireplace with a piece of yesterday's newspaper in front of her, but looking over the area with new eyes. A lot of people were going into the aerobics class, surprising at least when Cliff led them, that new man who thought he was training people for the Olympic gym team and who shouted at the slackers when they didn't bend over far enough. Annie and lots of other people seemed to enjoy the classes—walkers or not—although they liked Magda leading them a lot better. Carolina always felt a pang of guilt when she passed by the filled room, but she did pass by, quickly.

After aerobics, Sudoku and other word games were led by the aerobics teacher. These activities were to boost memory. The chairs that had been used for balance by those without walkers in the entertainment/aerobics room had to be rearranged for the noon movie that would be shown again at eight that night. The schedule for the day said the movie was *Kiss Me Kate*. Carolina read that men's poker was to be played in the afternoon and bridge in another room (the women had a hard time discouraging those who did not know they had forgotten how to play and had to disband and set up new teams often to shake them). Two days a week, Arts and Crafts was taught by the aerobics teacher. Every day was more or less the same thing except the movie changed. But Fridays were special with a glass of wine and entertainment at three.

Ah, yes, the entertainment. The same groups or individuals came to sing or play music for an hour. People got a drink beforehand. On Cinco de Mayo there was a mariachi band. Once in a while children came from a nearby dance studio to do a recital. One day there was a real singer from Ireland who sang and told the history of the "Troubles." That was great. They hired an opera singer from time to time who made one wish to hear that fire alarm again. If the canapés came late (usually little frankfurters or spinach in a pastry bought frozen from the supermarket), people would walk in front of the singer with their walkers to get them. The best entertainers were those who allowed the audience to sing along with them the old songs from their youth. Some people came to the entertainment to sleep, even though the sound system was so loud that people who could hear would keep shouting, "Turn it down" but to deaf ears. Being by a big city did give Management a pool of entertainers to draw from who performed "professionally" but cheap. Some of the Management had relatives who sang whom they called to give them a few bucks too.

A new couple came in the library with Fern, a marketing member. The couple seemed primed and ready. Fern brought them over to meet Carolina. "Maybe you can answer any of their questions." After being introduced to the couple and asking them to call her Carolina, the man asked "North or South?" Carolina cringed, usually men said that. "East," she said, "Northeast." The man was temporarily silenced. Then he tittered, "I'll bet your sisters are called Georgia and Virginia." Before Carolina could say anything, the woman asked what the retirement place was like.

"Pretty much what you see. It is good if you have family close."

"Oh, our children are ten minutes away."

The agent drew them away to see the dining room that was now about empty.

People started to come out of aerobics and late breakfast. Rolanda came out of the dining room with a friend. She went by with Rosemary who had permanently vacated the back table when Lillian came. It drove Margie crazy to see a well-dressed junior league type person like Rosemary with no memory, and repeating the same things every day, being accepted by Rolanda with smiles. But that is how it was. Lillian came in the library and sat down in another chair to prepare for her nap. Everyone who came out of their rooms made their way around the concierge desk looking for something like their papers or to sign up for grocery trips or the big trips they paid for to see plays and museums. Some went to do puzzles in the TV lounge/poker room. Aides were signing in and out. Staff were coming in to work and leaving. Management was having their meeting about the residents and how to manage them. Here was where the action was at this time of day.

Annie and Dot came in after aerobics and sat on the couch near Carolina. Milton and his wife came in and sat near Lillian. Even Rita came in as she saw her dining room companions in the library.

"Old home week," she said.

"All we need now is Margie," they said.

"I saw her in the office with Vito. I wonder if she is leaving. She can't seem to settle."

"Just so she doesn't come to our table." This comment was from Maxine. Everybody could hear the conversations in the library.

Conversation about Margie was about to break out in general when Margie herself bounced into the room. About three people stopped with their mouths open with comments they were about to make. Margie seemed happy for a change.

"Guess what?" she said.

"What?"

"I found an apartment. I am going to move in before I find anything wrong with it. It is next to the elevator but it is the best I can do. My furniture is coming. It is a two bedroom and I will sleep in the room farthest from the elevator. People don't use the elevator much at night anyway. Vito said maybe he can get the volume turned down on the elevator ding. It is louder than the one across from Annie and the one on the other side of the building on the first floor." (Margie knew every sound of the place.)

Carolina asked Margie to sit down in their growing circle to distract her from telling them the rest of the drawbacks of the apartment. Let her be happy about finding one. Maybe her wandering and inspecting would stop now.

Carolina quickly said, "Look at the menu for tonight." Most people were holding their copies of it in their hands after getting their memos from the Management.

Lillian yelled from behind them, "Yea, look! Ha! Turkey Marengo, Beef Wellington, and Fried Shrimp with Waffle Fries and Cole Slaw. What kind of menu is that?"

Rita said, "That food is going to kill us."

"Well, it is beef, poultry and sea food every day," Annie said.

Carolina rolled her eyes.

"One can always get the grilled chicken and salad from the side menu," Dot said.

"Have you tasted the grilled chicken? Dry as a bone." Lillian added, "That is NOT food!"

Annie asked, "What's 'Fish Wanda Cruz'?"

Lillian said, "That is a legitimate dish served in good restaurants. They should tell us about the jalapenos that are supposed to be in it."

Annie looked interested.

Carolina made a note to watch out for it with Annie and asked what they had had for breakfast. "Was it Danish day?"

"No, lox and bagels or waffles with whipped cream," Dot said.

Rita said, "I can't believe the menu here. Pastries and gravies and greasy stews. Salt is the ingredient you taste most in the soups. A lot of the soups they serve are thick cream soups. They have young guys here doing the menus who think fried shrimp is appropriate for old people with high cholesterol and blood pressure. They had sweet potatoes the other day, which is good for diabetics, but FRIED them. The heart healthy dish one night was fish drenched in fried bread crumbs. The other choices were lasagna with garlic bread and chicken pot pie with lots of thick crust and salt. They had potato pancakes as a side dish. Death by saturated fat."

"But you can get grilled chicken any day you want," Dot piped in again.

"That grilled chicken looks like they boil those frozen chicken patties they get," complained Margie.

Annie cut in with, "I love those potato pancakes."

"That is why they serve it. Give the people what they want and they'll beat a path to your door. They base their selections on a survey they took, although I don't think they listed the foreign sounding dishes," said Margie.

Dot remembered the soups from last week. "You are right, Rita. Last week they served cream of mushroom and cream of chicken and cheddar broccoli, which is sort of creamy."

"It is a miracle we all don't fall over after leaving the dining room. Some of these people are in their 90s. They must be made of iron," Carolina said.

"Good genetics," said Margie.

"What's for dessert tonight?" Annie asked.

"Cake with ice cream, sugar free fruit compote and cheesecake," Carolina read.

"I had that fruit compote and they put whipped cream on it from a can," said Rita. "The cream was not sugar free. The cookie was though."

Margie giggled. "Remember when they served 'Ham and Cheese Noodle Bake' or 'Quiche Lorraine' and 'Frito Pie' or 'Bratwurst on a Roll'? They came with onion rings, tater tots or cottage fries."

"Jesus," muttered Rita under her breath. "They're going to kill us, but why? They need residents."

This mention of killing was a mistake. It reminded Margie of a program she had seen about the end of the world: "Seven Ways the World Can End." She told the group about it. "A comet may hit us or there may be a gamma ray burst and we will die slowly in our basements or an earthquake will happen or a gigantic tsunami will over run the earth. Even a super swarm of locusts may bury our big cities." She saw that last on another show. "Let me see, what else can kill us?"

Carolina hurriedly said, "There's a lecture on the importance of fiber in our diet next week."

Rita snorted.

A heavy woman in a walker passed by and Margie commented, "That's my upstairs' neighbor, Shirley. I told her my husband had left me after 25 years and she laughed! She said she had been married 35 years and her husband left her for another woman. She couldn't have been happier. Her comment was 'no more meals to make for him.' She could do what she liked. Who understands people like that?" said Margie.

Margie added, "I got one of those calls today where no one talked."

Annie said, "I heard they're going around and on unlisted numbers, except for being in the directory here. Can't be kids. Is that what I was trying to think of? What's the movie today?"

"An old one," said Dot. "Why don't they get some new ones?"

Rita answered, "Angie, who orders them, says they get what people request. The request box is across from the elevator. I wonder if that's why they get the ones that were just on TCM. People forgot they just saw them on TV and request them."

Margie told them all she had to pack to move in.

"Are you coming to Happy Hour?" asked Carolina.

"Maybe not today. I usually get my glass of wine and don't go in. My furniture is coming any time now. It's good the elevator coverings are up since Ira moved out, or I would have to deal with Freddie. He would have some excuse for not putting them up. Wish me luck. I have to call the mover. Bye."

After she left, Dot said, "I'll believe she moves in when I see it. She's too scared to make a commitment."

"She made a commitment with her husband. We hear about it every day." Rita said sarcastically.

"Well, that's what men are like," said Dot.

"Not my man," said Annie sadly, missing her husband.

They stopped talking when they heard a commotion by the concierge desk. Angie, the jack-of-all-trades assistant to the other administrators, was calming down Joan, a resident, about the janitor, Freddie, who never showed up. A bulletin to look for him was issued. The visiting supreme head of the Courte was here today so Freddie was busy brownnosing. Anger in this place worried Carolina since it could signify the beginning of dementia in a person, but she was reassured when Freddie was mentioned because anger was called for.

"That Freddie," said Annie. "I don't trust him. He always blames the resident for the problem. Blanche said he came to fix the leaking pipe in her bathroom and blamed her for putting cleaning products under her sink. He said she broke the sink. We all have bottles under our sinks. We don't break anything."

A woman going by paused to say Freddie told her she probably ruined her dishwasher by using the wrong products and he made her show him. Then he told her she put the filter of her dryer in improperly when her clothes wouldn't dry. Of course it turned out to be a burnt out heating element.

"He's rude to almost everyone," said Lillian. "I don't care. I don't put up with it."

Carolina said, "Margie said she sees him coming out of empty apartments all of the time but they don't seem to get fixed for her to consider. I hope that is all over for her now."

Joan came over to get some moral support about Freddie. She was extremely upset. "All of the building supervisors I have ever met treat the facilities like people, and the people, especially elderly people, like they were toilet parts." (No one had ever heard this well-dressed lady talk like this before.) "Freddie barged in to look for some switch in my closet. I told him to wait until I got some things out of there. He plowed by and was in my walk–in closet, and next thing I saw, he had my urine test in his hand, which I grabbed out of his hand, saying give me back my urine test. He pushed my clothes around in batches while I grabbed the hat I was keeping on a box so it wouldn't get crushed before my nephew's wedding. Then he picked up my cash and will box that I don't want ANYONE to know I have. He found the switch and did something to it. The janitors will never understand the disrespect they perpetrate on us. I wrote a letter to the manager of this place about him but realized what a waste it would be to send it. Closets are where we keep our precious and private things. Four days later, they sent in two guys with Freddie to be shown where in selected apartments the important switches are. Off they marched into my closet again, pushing aside my personal things, while I rushed into the middle of them to show them where it was so they would leave. They then marched out again in a line while I stood looking to see if my newly pressed navy suit was injured in any way. I will never wear it like I used to. It has epaulettes on the shoulders." She looked wistful and lost.

Rita said, "He told me I made the washer leak from the bottom but I can't figure out how. One just has to accept that janitors hate tenants whom they think ruin their true love, the building, if one lives in these places."

"You have cash and personal papers in a box for anyone to carry out? You make it convenient for them," said Dot.

"I don't want my special things in a box in the bank since they close those safe deposit boxes to next of kin until authorities can get in to check it out for inheritance reasons. The box I have is fireproof so papers don't burn up. I didn't think anyone would steal it if no one knew it was there. Now they do. I don't know what to do. Life is too hard these days. My children will be mad I bought the box so I'm not telling them."

"Calm down," said Milton, who happened to go by. "I don't think the mean guy or his robots will take the box now that we all know it's there. But one of us may."

Everyone glared at him, some for scaring Joan and some for him implying they might be thieves. Milton decided his wife was calling him.

"And what is Angie doing here?" asked Rita, trying to change the subject. "She has the best designer clothes of any of us. I mean some of them you can tell were made for her. I heard her ex-husband was a bigtime lawyer and she had lots of jewels and was big in the social circuit."

"What do you mean ex? I heard she was married four times. She should be rich. She looks so good and she is near 60 but looks 40. What's she doing here? I know they get paid peanuts and she's just an assistant. She's very smart too." This from Dot.

Lillian answered, "Well, the good-looking bus driver is after her. I saw him rubbing her back the other day. Margie thinks he looks like a Greek god. I notice his clothes are immaculate, but I don't know about gods these days. I am beyond that and glad of it."

Rita got up to leave and they all went to their rooms for a rest or whatever.

Carolina rested for awhile, thinking that almost everyone seemed suspicious if you thought about them long enough. They all were guilty of something at sometime. *We are imagining things*, she thought. Is this the start of some shared dementia with Annie?

There was the Happy Hour at three o'clock. Right before three, Carolina went down for her glass of wine. There was already a line. Angie was serving the wine to residents. They were asking where the food was. Lots of them stuffed themselves at three, then wondered why they couldn't eat their four course meals at 4:30, first seating.

Carolina looked in the card room next to the video room. The music hour often disturbed the players. They seemed to take their poker seriously.

Carolina talked to a group of people. A new entertainer was coming today. The food was late as usual, planned so Management didn't have to serve too much?

People started to file into the video room to get good seats. Walkers were a problem in that room if too many people came. Carolina sat in the back to see everyone in front of her—how they were grouped and if there were any disagreements, to see who wasn't there. She had picked up a puffed something from a tray on the way in. Annie came in and sat by her and Dot on the other side. The poker group broke up, Carolina thought, because some wanted to see the new singer. Ike sat with his girlfriend, whose daughter had brought her over. The place was full. Milton was there to sing along. There were calls for more food. Lillian actually loved these probably recently frozen hors d'oeuvres. She was one of those who stuffed herself with this mess at three and wondered why she couldn't eat her four course dinner at four. Life was incomprehensible to Carolina. She hoped they would stop serving them before the singer started. It was embarrassing when the people got up in front of him or her to grab food. Walkers had to be pushed out of the way for the people to get up in the small aisles. It was so distracting. Most of the singers were older and looked a bit seedy, like old bachelor middle-school band teachers paid badly, with their sense of pitch ruined by 20 years of hearing "music" by 11-year-olds who had never heard of John Philip Sousa.

Today's singer was setting up his gear and testing. He was dressed as a symphony conductor. He began. In a thick accent, he said he had just come from Russia. The volume was always set too loud in this small room. There were going to be shouts of "Turn it down!" He announced his song and began, "Funiculi-Funicula...." Most people didn't find a man singing an Italian song with a thick Russian accent funny. Carolina wondered what it sounded like to an Italian. Margie had come in late. She did find it funny. She had a sense of humor but nobody noticed unless she said something really funny. They took every remark of hers, however tongue-in-cheek, seriously.

The singer finished, bowed abruptly and said "Thank you very much" in a clipped way. Margie thought, *Andy Kauffman is not dead. He is alive and playing a joke on people in an old folks home.* The singer announced his next song, "La Cucaracha," and bowed. His long hair fell down as he did, showing his large bald spot on the top of his head. He was sweating a lot. He invited people to sing along, at least that is what Carolina thought he said. She found it funny not to laugh at this group trying to sing "La Cucaracha" in this crowded room on these plastic chairs with walkers all over the place where people had no real homes. He finished the song alone. He bowed in a clipped way again and said, "Thank you very much."

Then he did a version of a Blues' song he he said saw Muddy Waters doing on TV. The only words anyone could understand were "Don't say I don't love you, just 'cause I don't treat you right." Margie was moving to the jazz beat and shaking her head mournfully.

The next song he announced was "My Way"— a Frank Sinatra hit. Was only Carolina suppressing a laugh? She looked over at Margie who was now actually laughing. His words were unintelligible, except for a few. At first, Carolina thought he was singing in Russian or Italian or some foreign language. People did sing along; they loved Frank and knew his songs. This was followed by lots of clapping and preening with relief on the singer's part. He asked them to please ask Management to have him back, to request him again. He seemed desperate in his sweating, trying way. Poor people trying to earn a dollar.

He then announced his next song. He was going to sing "You Ain't Nothin' But a Hound Dog" by Elvis Presley. He said he loved Elvis Presley. (Margie was hiding her face, laughing in the napkin left over from her little hot dog puff thing.) The Russian émigré not only sang the words with his thick accent but danced to Elvis' "Hound Dog."

The crowd burst out clapping after his abrupt, "Thank you very much," and formal bow. He was sweating like he was in the shower. He mopped his face with a cloth hanky.

Then everything stopped. The door opened and a person in a wheel chair insisted on coming in. Chairs had to be moved and people changed seats to make room for her.

After this, someone shouted "Do 'Danny Boy.'" The singer stared and, believe it or not, turned his back on them—Carolina thought he was overcome with insult or disappointment—but he was not. He walked over to the piano in the corner. He sat down with his back to the audience but turned his head around as much as he could so the audience could see his face, and sang "Danny Boy," beautifully played. It was not funny anymore. It was moving—his desire to please, his musicianship, his unknown and seemingly sad life, to be here with us. He ended. The hour was up. He got up, moved to the middle of the room and he bowed then for a longer time. "Thank you very much." He was very emotional. People were getting up and leaving, but he was asking them to take his card and handing them out in his sweating hand. *Poor dear man,* Carolina thought. She got up, took his card and thanked him for his wonderful show. He grabbed her hand and kissed it. Why did she think then, *Why doesn't he wash his hair?* It was so she wouldn't cry, she hoped.

They all left slowly, held up by the exit again. Another walker brigade.

Annie walked out with her. She seemed sad. She said to Carolina, "I wonder how long I am signed up here for?"

Carolina said, "You will still be asking me that in 10 years."

Annie said with fervor, "No, I won't."

She told Carolina that the monthly bulletin had come out listing birthdays and hers was not in it. Carolina could see she was crestfallen. "I want a big party like Beverly had with a big cake for everyone. I will ask my children if I can have it. I will be 90. Why did the place leave me off the list?"

Carolina said, "It was a mistake. There was another Ann on it and they probably made an error and listed only one."

Annie lamented, "People will not go around wishing me a happy birthday like they will the people on the list."

That was true. Poor friend. Maybe they could put a notice on the concierge desk.

Dinner time came for the first seaters. Annie and Carolina went up to their rooms to wash their hands (i.e., use the toilet) and came back down. The file into the dining room began quickly. Coming in wasn't a problem for the first seaters. Each one sat down and prayed the assigned people would show up in time or else ordering dinner would be held up until all parties were present. Carolina, Annie, Dot, Lillian and Rita were all accounted for. They were waiting for Margie who was usually the first person there.

Wearing a colorful turban, Dot said, "Did you hear? *Kiss Me Kate* didn't come in from Netflix. They sent *Melinda, Melinda* instead. Very sexy. Everyone left."

Carolina nodded. That fitted in with her theory that sex was not rampant in this old folks home. She was glad when Dot wore her more flamboyant hats instead of the few gloomy ones she owned.

Dot added, "Of course, no men had shown up for the noon movie. We'll see how many show up at eight after the word gets out."

"Oh," thought Carolina, deflated.

They looked at the menu, hopeless until Margie showed up. Lillian remarked how ridiculous it was they couldn't order until the last person showed up. She said she had seen another diner at one of the tables here order seltzer, tomato juice, coke and coffee and never touched any of them. They were present on the table when he came in every day. "I am going to do that too."

"Try it!" laughed Annie.

Finally Margie came in with a hangdog look and sat in her seat. She said she had signed the lease on her apartment and had been lectured on her behavior by the marketing guy. He said she had been removed before from a dining table at someone's request. He said people complained that she was too negative. "This young kid lectured me, a woman over twice his age, and he doesn't even know the circumstances! I hate him. And he's taking $50,000 while he does it! I wonder how much he makes that he can be so superior. He knows I'm in a hard place emotionally or he wouldn't act like that. I'm humiliated. I have even failed nursing home. And the new apartment is next to the elevator like I said I hated. It's next door to Ike except for the elevator. We will be alone in that whole wing except for the dancer in the corner."

Comforting words didn't help.

The server came by. Some of the servers didn't care about service, some were mean on purpose, but some tried very hard to please, an impossible ambition here. Tonight one of the pleasers took the order, an heroic stance in this land of some picky seniors. Lillian told her the new permanent drink order she wanted in front of her every night, the same as Mr. Widdoes (the near celebrity who had known Rockefeller, Nelson). The server said yes. (Wait until the Dining Room Manager heard.) Carolina hoped it wouldn't cause retaliation by one of the mean servers on another night, actually day, with dinner at 4:30. Then the ordering came.

"What's in Beef Marco Polo?" asked Annie?

"I don't know," said the server, "I'll ask."

This meant the server going to the kitchen. She might be intercepted by another table and not come back for ages. Carolina hated when someone asked what was in the food. The servers never knew.

"I'll get the Fried Shrimp with Waffle Fries," said Dot, a woman with high blood pressure and diabetes.

"What is the chicken?" asked Annie, knowing full well fried fish was her favorite.

"Turkey Marengo," read Margie.

Out of character, Carolina said, "Don't ask or we'll never eat and they will make us leave before we are ready and take the tablecloth away again."

The server came back, all ordered the irresistible fried shrimp with waffle fries and cole slaw, even Rita. The server reported on what was in the Marco Polo. And she had come back, bringing a tray with seltzer, tomato juice, coke and coffee on it. Everyone at the table marveled at Lillian. (But wait for tomorrow.) She hardly touched them during her meal. She said she would be up all night going to the bathroom if she did. She added querulously, "How can I be expected to eat this much? They gave us all that stuff to eat at Happy Hour!" The "gourmet" just gobbled that junk up but complained about her dinner!

Milton's voice came to the diners very loudly telling one of his jokes. He looked at his wife and said, "We have been married, dear, for 67 years. Thank you for the best 13 years of my life!"

"What did he say?" Lillian asked.

"He said he was happiest when he was 13," Annie answered.

"I don't get it."

Conversation continued as the courses came. Rita got aluminum foil in her soup but thought it was useless to complain about it. Lillian complained for her, unpleasantly, to the server, but it was useless. Carolina was surprised the servers hadn't poisoned them all by now. The servers were blamed for a lot of the chef's misdeeds.

Annie asked Rita if she had gotten anything good on eBay lately.

"I did bid on a Spode teapot; it is the very one they use on the PBS series everyone is watching, the upstairs people use it, of course. I had to bid separately on matching Spode teacups to go with it. And the worst happened. I got the cups but not the teapot."

Carolina made a harrumphing sound. So that was why those teacups were in the trash room the other day she thought but said nothing. The others noticed her sign of disapproval but didn't say anything.

Margie hated silences and filled them in. She said the table with Rolanda was not the only table where she did not feel welcome. She was seated at the one behind us with the three men and three women when one of the women had not come one night. Margie replaced her. She told that group about news items she had recently seen on TV, one being about Teflon killing parrots in kitchens from the fumes Teflon gives off at high heat and the other being about how some people who get hit on the head permanently talk with foreign accents. "They're true facts but they wouldn't believe me!"

"I don't either," said Annie.

Margie, ruffled by the remark, continued: "And one of the men said that Neil Simon had written *Blithe Spirit* but I told him it was Noel

Coward. I sat at that other table another night with the guy who knew Rockefeller, and he said Philip Roth had written *Love Story*. I said it was Eric Segal. He said nothing until later in the dinner when he tried to explain away his mistake." Margie remembered that he soon left the table that night and she never got to eat there again.

Poor Margie, thought Carolina, *people don't like to be corrected.*

Annie suddenly said, "I'm moving to Florida. I haven't told my children yet. I shouldn't have to pass another winter in the cold."

Carolina suddenly turned cold. She looked at her friend with concern. What was happening? Her children would never let her go to Florida. It was disturbing.

Suddenly, there were red flashing lights on one side of the dining room that flashed throughout the room. Conversation stopped at "Who is it?" Every few weeks diners were faced with seeing their future if they were here long enough. Carolina thought, one day that ambulance will be for each of us. Some of us have already had that ride but came back. Carolina could feel the fear in the room. How many times can one come back?

Margie quickly said, "I watched NOVA the other night and we may be two dimensional people in a hologram on the edge of the universe near a black hole. Or according to string theory, we may suddenly be attacked by nothingness, there will instantaneously be nothing."

Then one of the chef's came out to talk to the table, the chef with the dirty shirt and pajama pants with figures on them and the turned around baseball cap that infuriated Annie. He had his hands on his hips. He smirked and she fumed. He said, "I heard you had a problem with the soup." Lillian spoke up for Rita about the aluminum foil.

"It must have been the servers," he said and shrugged.

Annie asked him if he cared.

He answered, "Not really."

After he left, Carolina thought the conversation had become depressing and morbid. She suggested they leave. A lot of other people had had the same idea, and there was a long slow line leaving while the ambulance lights still flashed. She decided to follow Annie to see what was wrong with her.

CHAPTER EIGHT—A TALK WITH ANNIE

Carolina asked Annie if she wanted to go up to her room for a quiet evening. Annie said, "yes, come to my room." They went up. Carolina noticed that Annie's door was not locked again. Annie's daughter was supposed to talk to her about it. They went in and sat side by side on comfortable living room recliners with a small table between them.

They talked about tonight's dinner and that chef who was about 20 and had worked in a fast food burger place before he came here. "I'll bet he doesn't know what a Michelin star is," remarked Carolina.

"A what?" asked Annie.

"A food rating," said Carolina. "How are you feeling?"

"I'm tired today."

It was companionable to rest in their chairs without talking or listening to TV, just two old ladies, sharing a common friendship and age. They didn't have to tell each other about their common pains.

Annie said she was feeling confused today. She talked about the day she had run into Carolina while she was going to the exit to wait for her daughter who was coming to take her to the Doctor. Her daughter liked to use that exit, although it was farther from Annie's room. Annie had been looking at something, and then Carolina came up behind her, and Annie's daughter came to the locked entrance door to be let in. Then two policemen with Angie came in behind her daughter. Angie let them all in with her FOB. "They passed by us, except my daughter, and went off to the offices. I remember staring at something. But what and why?"

"Was anybody else in the hall?" asked Carolina. Carolina remembered but she wanted Annie to say what she saw to get a fresh view of the incident.

"I passed Nadia with her cleaning cart. Then I saw Dot was there without her walker. That was the only time I have seen her outside her apartment without it."

"Me too," said Carolina. "She turned around when she saw the police coming. I wonder if she wanted to go to the library to hear what the rumors were about why they came or if she had something to say to police. She never said, and I didn't think about it afterwards. We tend not to remember things here, not to mention our shorter attention spans. I have noticed I don't even remember little disagreements that I would have remembered in the past. The past is past as far as our near memories are concerned. It's good in some ways, isn't it? We begin each day anew, unless something has happened that is either really good or really bad."

Annie agreed. She said she was glad to get this memory off her chest. If only she could remember what she was thinking in that hall.

"What about going to Florida?"

"Oh, that. I got carried away. I know I'm not going to Florida or anyplace else except my daughter's home for dinner. It was like a dream that was real when I said it."

Carolina thought, *who knows the stages of different sorts of memory loss? I have seen countless ways and paths of it. They don't fit the official definitions perfectly. I could tell these psychologists a few things myself, a million shades of memory loss. How is that for a title of a bestseller?*

Annie was speaking. "I wasn't called from that last bridge club list I signed up for. I'm a good bridge player. I was waiting for a call and then saw them already playing. They didn't tell me."

"Don't take it hard. Sometimes they have their own clique. Those board games are more fun and just as good. You're good at them. Card numbers are hard to remember. Lots of us can't do it anymore and the players down there are fierce. Most people aren't in their league."

"I never had trouble before," said Annie.

"We're still independent. Let's be happy for that. I remember I liked to climb the ladder to pick apples from my tree at my house. Then I couldn't. It's harder with our memories, though. We have to enjoy what's left and we have a lot left."

Annie smiled and agreed. She was a realistic old girl.

"You remember the words to those old songs better than I do," said Carolina.

"I know," Annie laughed.

Carolina got up to leave. She was tired. "Well, I'm off. See you tomorrow."

She went to her wing. Margie had moved to the opposite wing. Carolina thought she should go over to ask if she could help since no family was here to help Margie, but she couldn't. Help, that is. She needed to lie down. She was tired physically and spiritually, but she knew help would always be available to her in silence. She was glad for a moment to be in a place where everything is close or would be after taking one of the elevators. She got to her room and unlocked it. She went in and then stood in shock. There were black sooty footprints in the middle of the hall to the bedroom starting at her entrance. The stride seemed to be wide like a man's. Carolina checked to see if her valuables were taken but everything seemed to be there. She checked the bottoms of her shoes to see if she had stepped in something before, as unlikely as that was, but the bottoms were clean. She went in to sit on the couch. Why would someone come into her apartment and not take anything? Did they know she was looking for something suspicious around here? But she didn't tell anyone or know what it was, so why would anyone suspect her of having any suspicions concerning the Courte? Carolina got up to put up the chain on her door now that she knew no one else was in the apartment. She wondered why the Management let them keep a chain on the door when they had keys to get in in an emergency but not to the chain. She thought the chain was flimsy and easily cut, maybe that was why. It gave residents a false sense of security. She turned to get ready for bed early when she stopped. There was now a line of soot from the hall to the couch where there hadn't been a little while ago. It couldn't be. It had to be a ghost, but she didn't think they left black tracks.

She sat down again. Now, she thought, *I'm losing my mind* (different from losing one's memory). Her feet hurt. She took off her thick wedge shoes and suddenly looked more carefully at one of them. The wedge part on the side had a crack in it. She looked inside. The foam or whatever the black wedge part was made of was disintegrating. When she pushed on the heel the hole opened and she saw black soot. The hole closed when she did not bend it. That was why she hadn't seen it when she lifted each foot separately to check the bottoms of her shoes before. And that was why she had thought it was a man with a big stride- because it was only one shoe that made the marks. She was stalking herself! Her carpet color was light while the carpet in the hall was navy, so she hadn't seen her footprints leading to or away from her apartment outside her door. She collapsed in laughter and relief.

She said aloud, "I'm going to bed.   After I vacuum."

CHAPTER NINE—MARGIE SPEAKS (AND SPEAKS)

"Oh, no!" Carolina opened her eyes. She hurt from tiredness. "I'm not going, alarm or no alarm. I'm going to put those ear plugs in my ears and go back to bed. Or go see Annie who never goes because she can't do the stairs. Why is this happening?"

She put both feet out and pushed herself up. She looked for her clothes. She'd thrown her wedge shoes out and now had only bedroom slippers under her bed. She couldn't walk down the steps in those. She might fall. She looked for shoes in the closet. "No wonder I may be imagining things with this going on. We need rest. Maybe there is a fire?" Then, "I have to set a good example for the others." Out she went and down the steps. She walked through the fire doors and then to the lobby, meeting people near the main desk on the first floor filing out. Margie was already out there with the usual gang. The fire department showed up with their flashing lights. Flashing lights everywhere.

People mumbled that they would have to leave if this kept up. Conversation in general popped up.

"How did the moving go, Margie? Did you get everything? Did the alarm scare you awake?"

"It's alright. I was up all night unpacking, my stuff came early. Nobody is below or across from or under me or anywhere around me but upstairs, so it's OK to make noise. Ike is next to me but the elevator is between us. I can't sleep much anyway."

Poor girl, Carolina thought, *Insomnia too.* Aloud she said to everyone, "By the way, how full was the room for *Melinda, Melinda*?"

"Empty. A few men showed up and left."

Carolina beamed. Her theory about the place was right. She hoped she wasn't a prude; of course, she wasn't.

"How's your cat, Margie?"

"Oh, not so good. She stares and jumps and stays near the door watching and waiting for something to happen. She stares at something like it's moving and cowers. I think she wants to go home. I do too."

"I thought you were getting divorced and left to get away," said Maxine.

"I did but I didn't want the divorce."

People looked embarrassed.

"OK to go in folks," said the firefighter as the alarm went silent. The tip from the concierge, by way of Ike, was that there was no reason for the alarm again.

Margie left singing that Bonnie Rait song to herself "I Can't Make You Love Me If You Don't." Did she mean her husband or the people at the Courte?

The next day, everybody seemed to be cranky, missing most activities.

Carolina made her way to dinner again. Margie walked in, taking her seat. Carolina wanted to just eat and go. Is eating dinner in an hour too much to ask just once in a while?

Annie asked if they all got their calendars from the Management with a Norman Rockwell picture on each page. Everyone said yes. Annie didn't think Carolina's response was enthusiastic enough. "Don't you love Norman Rockwell, Carolina?"

"Well, not particularly, since you asked."

Annie got angry and said, "You're not American if you don't like Norman Rockwell!"

Carolina was startled. She said, "He's okay, but I have other favorites."

Annie seemed calmed down, but it didn't look like another cozy evening of retirement home bonding for her and Carolina.

The server came and they ordered, five orders of Chicken Diablo and one Haddock Florentine.

"What the heck is in Diablo?" Lillian asked the server. She was in a bad mood too. "And where are my seltzer, tomato juice, coke and coffee?"

The server snapped, "I'll get your drinks later. There are other tables to serve too."

Lillian didn't say anything. This response from a server probably rated a visit to the Head Manager tomorrow. The server left and Lillian repeated, "I didn't get an answer, but what's in Diablo? I never saw it served at Sardi's."

Margie said, "Did you know there's an app for that?"

Lillian looked at her blankly.

Margie stammered, "You know, to tell you what's in dishes." She changed the subject— wishing again to have a grandchild before she died.

Unfortunately, that didn't work to keep pleasant conversation going, so she said, "I walked outside today and saw lots of worms on the sidewalk. Why were they there? I'd heard they have to escape drowning in the ground but it was not rainy today. It looked like mass suicide to me. I had to spend an hour putting them back on the grass." (And she wondered why people thought she was peculiar.)

"That was very kind of you," said Carolina, "You should look it up on your computer." The other women exchanged looks like Margie was nuts.

The courses of food came and the tablemates ate in silence except for remarks by Margie.

Of course she would talk about cat food. "I saw a package of cat treats today that said in big letters that it contained 'taurine.' How is that for advertising? Who knew cats needed taurine and who would go out to buy it without commercials? When I was a kid, cats ate scraps from the table all of the time. Of course, they disappeared every few years and we got new cats, so we never knew if their diet was bad or not. Things are better for them now, of course, spaying and all that."

Even Margie saw this conversation was going nowhere, so she changed to what had happened to her last night. "You know these retirement places are confusing. They have all of those gadgets to call for help in the bathroom so you can't use both sides of your sink. I used to put my toothpaste tube and hydrocortisone cream for, you know, hemorrhoids on separate sides of the sink, but I can't now. Last night I got them mixed up and ended up brushing my teeth with hydrocortisone cream and using the toothpaste on my butt. That mint really burns. I blame my husband."

There were no comments from anyone. Margie tried again.

"I had the TV on while I was unpacking and can't keep up with these new scientific theories of the universe. There is a weak force and dark energy and dark matter and particles that do strange things. They said the whole universe may be alive and reproducing itself. There is evidence that it spawns more universes at the bottom of black holes. A physicist on one of the talk shows said there is no need for a God concept now."

Everyone looked shocked. Even Margie knew she had said something wrong. "I didn't say it. God is fine with me!"

Another course being served saved her.

"Who is that man way over by the pictures there?" (He was half of the "ideal" couple Carolina had heard bickering so ferociously.) "He got in the elevator today on my floor and hissed 'fatso' under his breath. I know he meant me to hear. I'd even held the elevator door for him until he got there with his walker and I said "Hello." Margie looked like she was going to cry.

"Are you sure you heard right?" asked Annie.

"We have heavy burdens to bear here and people can sometimes be mean from pain," Carolina said.

Dot asked if we'd seen *Little House on the Prairie* on TV. "It's on right before we come down to eat. We miss the ending by 15 minutes. I love Michael Learned."

Margie interrupted. "You mean Karen Grassle. She plays the mother. Michael Learned plays the mother on *The Waltons*." Margie couldn't help correcting Dot in her quest for informational perfection.

Dot glared at Margie.

"They look so much alike," Carolina quickly interjected.

However, Margie couldn't shut up. Carolina thought it was part of her medical condition. It got worse when she was worked up or dizzier than usual. She'd said something about that happening sometimes. Why couldn't she just be quiet?

Margie went off again, although her comments had not been a great success up to now. "See that table behind us? (Milton's) That new woman asked me if my husband was alive since I keep talking about what he said, but she commented that she didn't see him here. I told her, 'Yes, unfortunately, he isn't dead. He replaced me by using the internet. Men can advertise these days and get just what they want—like a steak made to order.' She won't talk to me now. It's not like we can't say the words 'divorce' or 'menopause' these days, is it?"

From the looks she got from everyone, Margie must have realized it was. "I like Norman Rockwell!" she lied.

Annie, who was still evidently miffed at Carolina, smiled and asked Margie if she would go upstairs to her room with her after dinner. Maybe she would like a glass of wine.

The last that Carolina saw of them that night was Margie with her arm around Annie's neck going up to Annie's apartment while they sang, "Show Me the Way to Go Home."

Carolina went to her room grumpier than ever, not believing what a horrible day it had been.

She didn't know that tomorrow would top anything for horrible that she had experienced yet.

CHAPTER TEN—IT FINALLY HAPPENS

Carolina woke the next day thinking, "I'm going to Florida." She got up, stretched, said her prayers and smiled. I'm a silly old woman with friends and all I could want of comfort. I should live more austerely really. It's up to me to make a home and to be a support to my fellow creatures. I hope Annie is over her snit too. Carolina made breakfast and prepared for her walk. She had an outing planned to her friends' home in the country tomorrow including a visit with her beloved animals. She wanted to be ready for it.

She had to do her hair today to be ready for tomorrow.   Carolina got her hair cut professionally but managed it herself. She had dark gray hair crimped nicely into fashionable waves—fashionable for the 1930s, that is. She wore it all of her life in the style her mother had adopted when Carolina was a child. She thanked God for modern hair gel. She really did. These days she'd wash her hair every few days, apply a stiffening gel to it and finger wave it, forming curls with her hands and then using metal rods with prongs on the end that clamped together to crimp the hair into tight waves. One couldn't sleep on these curlers, of course, but they were better than the old fashioned permanents women would get with metal curlers connected with long wires to a machine that burned the hair into curls and burned one's head too. Her mother had started these permanents for Carolina when she was five. By the time they were removed in the 1950s, she could tell the difference immediately between burning hair and burning scalp and scream for help. (One couldn't just pull the curlers from your hair or your hand would be burnt too.) She had tried chemical permanent waves but a few early ones had burned her scalp worse than the old machines that looked like electrocution devices, and the chemical treatments had made her hair fall out in patches. She was thinking of giving them another try. Maybe they'd improved them in the last fifty years.

She sat for a while waiting for the gel to dry, lost in thought about what she had to do for the day and, well, just lost in thought. She must remember to take sunblock with her in case she had to be out in the sun long at the block party— in the old days called a fete. Her skin was tanned from not using sunblock all of those years—who did in her day? Sunblock was a relatively new idea (considering her age), and she had not been one to wear hats out on her adventures, although she did when she'd gardened in the afternoons at her home, but she usually gardened in the evenings.

Oh, those adventures. Being a teacher and having the summers off meant she had time to travel but not much money. She remembered the times that she and her friends would take old tramp steamers that took a few passengers for extra money as they delivered their cargo in remote parts of the world. She saw ports in South America that way. Sometimes an old black and white "B" movie would remind her of those days. There were no stabilizers or fancy columns on those ships, she thought. Seasick females just leaned over the side or cleaned up their cabins as sailors laughed at them. They surely were a tougher breed then. And the sailors! She could tell a few tales about them too to young people, although they treated the (paying) women with respect, as long as the sailors weren't drunk. But the teachers took care of each other and anyone else misunderstanding women travelling alone. But Carolina had lots of chores to do today.

Her apartment was to be cleaned today. The service was provided every other week, probably to make sure there were no real problems with residents' hoarding or not taking care of their apartments. The women who cleaned had schedules that covered 365 days a year, not that they worked 365 days, but the schedules covered every day, even for part timers, except for weekends. One poor woman with a family, who had since left, showed up at Carolina's on Thanksgiving once. It was a Thursday, after all. She said if she didn't show up, she didn't get paid. It made scheduling easy. They came in the apartment if you were there or not unless you said no, and then you missed that service for a whole month. Most staff members, except administrators, were from other countries. Nadia was the cleaner assigned to Carolina's apartment. Carolina liked being there when she came but left the room being cleaned to give Nadia privacy. Some people were known to be very demanding, but the cleaners did their best to please. One cried once to Carolina since her hours were being, cut and she was afraid she'd offended a resident somehow for refusing to do her windows, which wasn't allowed. On the other hand, Carolina had walked in with a friend to the friend's apartment to see the cleaner using the toilet brush in the kitchen sink. Probably she had used it on everything. So Carolina liked to be there. The cleaner was coming at two and leaving at three, but Carolina had a lot to do that day to keep her busy in her apartment. Nadia came and propped the door open and left an enormous heavy cart in the hall loaded with cleaning supplies and a vacuum.

Nadia and Carolina talked a bit. "How is your brother?" "He has a job now." etc. They didn't discuss the incident where Nadia was caught by her husband, who was visiting between taxi runs, locked in the staff bathroom with one of the workmen here. Residents of one side of the building heard the fracas until Nadia drove away. That incident gave them something to talk about for a week. Nadia must have had a good explanation since husband and wife were spotted still talking together from time to time.

Three residents at Carolina's table—Dot, Annie and Rita—were also assigned Nadia as their cleaner. The poor cleaners did not do apartments in a row but had to drag their carts all over the building depending on which apartment they were assigned, location not being a factor. Nadia left with a smile and a forbidden tip, and the rest of the day belonged to Carolina. She was preparing all of the things she had bought for the friends she was to visit—human and not—special treats. She felt guilty for not baking something instead of ordering these goodies online. Well, she justified herself by thinking that ingredients were expensive to keep if one didn't use them a lot.

She went downstairs to see Annie reading her newspaper in the library. She sat down beside her at the reading table and picked up a piece of the paper provided by the home.

"Here, take some of mine, that one's missing a lot," Annie said.

The women smiled and shared Annie's paper. Carolina didn't say anything about last night but Annie did.

"After that glass of wine, Margie got really upset. She kept asking what Rolanda had against her and kept saying she should go up to her apartment and ask her. She said Rolanda still looked at her with pure, pure hatred at breakfast when she ran into her. I suggested that the incident was all over and she seemed happy at our table. Did I do the right thing?"

"Oh, yes. Assertiveness is good, but we must discourage confrontations with each other here, especially for Margie. She'll get a worse reputation and might be asked to leave. Good job, Annie." Annie's usual air of cheerfulness had returned.

Joyce, the dignified woman who'd helped Margie with her bastard comment on Margie's husband, sat down. She said she might have to move. She said her rent increase was too high and it was added on to the rent that had been high when she moved here. "I asked for a reduction of the increase, but they said they'd only give me a 2% reduction of the increase which was triple that. That's laughable. They think the old timers will stay here forever."

The group talked about the unfair increases and wondered at the logic of Management who were charging the new people so much less. They'd thought it was for the hard-to-rent apartments, but that didn't seem to be the way it was working out from what people had let slip, but that was not verified. The group believed them though.

"I may get a good fixed income but it *is* fixed," said Joyce. "I have to cut down on things I used to buy and it's just getting too tight now. I have more co-pays with Medicare now that I'm older and have more illnesses. You know how it goes."

The other two nodded. Joyce left.

Annie and Carolina were ready to leave when Floyd walked over to them. Annie was showing Carolina a rash on her arm. Margie was going by and said, "I've got an ointment for you to rub on. I'll go get it," and left. Floyd was in one of his "performing" modes, flirting with Annie who enjoyed it. He suddenly opened his belt and acted like he was going to open his zipper and said, "Here, I'll give you something to rub!" Then he left. Carolina was offended. Annie, however, thought it was the funniest thing she'd ever seen and laughed for five minutes straight!

Margie came back with a tube of cream and Annie rubbed the ointment on. Rolanda came up to the concierge desk in front of the open library. Margie sat slumped in her seat with her back to the long concierge counter. Apparently, she was in hiding today, not having had any wine. Rolanda gave instructions to the concierge to tell the cleaner Nadia not to come to her apartment today.

"Are you going somewhere for long?" (Residents were supposed to report long absences.)

"No, I'm not going anywhere today. I just don't want cleaning today. My daughter is coming." She left.

The concierge left the area for about ten minutes after that, probably trying to get the news to Nadia who was scheduled to be cleaning another apartment then.

"Look," said Annie, "anyone could come in and go anywhere they want without being questioned. I'll be more careful to lock my door from now on."

Unexpectedly, three people came in: Lillian's dentist son, his well-dressed wife and his well-dressed daughter. The little girl wore a designer dress, a Gucci purse over her arm and heels as high as they made them in her size for ten-year-olds. She seemed born for an old age home. She looked and sounded just like her grandmother. Carolina wanted to eat with them to see if the little girl knew her gourmet dishes and would announce "This is NOT food!"

"She had to have been cloned," said one of the gossipers whose identity will be kept secret at her request. They looked at the little family group that was whisking Lillian, their surprisingly loved relation, off to their home—or to some fancy restaurant.

Margie added, "Scientists worked so hard to clone her?" (Pause) "I guess I'm mean because I'm jealous. I want a grandchild. I want one different from me, though. I have to go. I'll tell you at dinner about Megaflares and our planet."

They looked at her blankly. She often made unconnected statements out of nowhere.

Margie got up to leave. "Can I get in trouble for just looking sad?"

Carolina stayed about fifteen minutes longer and got up to leave herself. She heard screaming and ran as fast as she could in the direction of the hall the scream was coming from. She met Carrie Ann who was in the hall walking towards the exit door. Margie had just gotten out of the elevator and was running down the corridor towards them. They rushed to her as fast as they could go. She fell as she got to them, and they each supported her by an arm and walked down the hall, making their way to the main desk.

As they got to the corner to go to the other corridor, they heard a shout behind them: "Is everything OK?" Shirley had come in the locked side door with two friends, using her fob to get in.

Carolina shouted back, "I don't think everything is OK yet, but we don't need help."

The small group that had come in, got on the elevator to their floor. Carolina, Carrie Ann and Margie continued on to the front desk.

A crowd collected as Margie was deposited in front of the concierge desk in a chair. Margie kept repeating, "She's dead, she's dead, she's dead..." Someone brought her water and she sipped some. The concierge came out along with people from the offices. The concierge asked, "Who?"

"Rolanda."

"Where?"

"In her room. Hurry!"

A driver and a repairman with a key were sent on up.

Rolanda's daughter came in the front door. Margie started to yell, "Don't go up. Your mother's dead, your mother's dead!"

The daughter, a middle aged blond woman, stood speechless and looked stunned.

A phone call came to the concierge desk, apparently from the men who had gone upstairs. "Dead?" (Pause) "I'll call the police." (Pause) "Stay with her until someone comes up. Is anyone in the apartment?" (The concierge was getting instructions from administrators who had come from the back offices.)

The concierge called 911. "A body. Send an ambulance and the police... I'll make sure nobody else enters, but watches the door... I don't know... A resident. She came to the desk to report it, but she's hysterical... She's not going anywhere...."

Freddie was sent to go up to Rolanda's apartment to watch the door and to get the other people out. It seemed as soon as he was gone, an ambulance with flashing lights came along with an emergency vehicle and a car full of police. Angie took them up to Rolanda's apartment. Rolanda's daughter was told to wait.

Carolina supposed they did the things they were supposed to do with crime scenes. One officer stayed behind to question the concierge and get information on what had happened so far. Rolanda's daughter said she was going up. She was told not to. Wait. The officer got a call from upstairs. Rolanda's daughter insisted that she was going up but was prevented by staff standing in front of the elevator. The officer asked them if the daughter could sit in a room. They took her to the office.

"Who found her?"

They pointed to Margie. He wrote down her name. He asked the staff to take her to another room away from Rolanda's daughter and stay with her.

A man and woman came in dressed in suits and everyone knew they were detectives. The staff gave the officer on the first floor directions and the detectives were taken to Rolanda's apartment.

Carolina sat with Margie in a copy room behind the big office. Police matters took place—the body identified, places taped off, crime scene people came and went. Margie was allowed to go to her room with a policewoman. Carolina went with her. Before they left, Carolina asked that they look up her records and tell Margie's son to come as soon as he could.

Margie lay on her couch. Carolina and the policewoman took chairs. They waited.

Margie was still hysterically crying but Carolina didn't ask her questions since there was a witness present.

"Should we call a doctor?" Carolina asked.

"No, wait until the detective comes," said the policewoman.

Eventually, a woman detective came to the apartment. She came in and took charge. She asked Margie to sit up. She asked the policewoman to take notes.

Margie said, "She's dead. I know she's dead."

"Yes, she is. You found her?"

"Yes, I went upstairs and saw her door propped open. I went in to see Rolanda on the floor in her living room. I bent over to see if I could help her and saw she was dead. Blood everywhere. The knife…"

"Did you take a knife up there?"

"Me, no! What do you mean?"

"Where did you see the body?"

"Beyond the foyer and the little kitchenette that's to the right. You could see her from the door."

"Did you see anybody?"

"No, not from the elevator to Rolanda's apartment. There was no one."

"Then what?" asked the detective.

"I got scared. What if the killer was in the bedroom or bathroom? I was going to get up to run for help when Gwen came in and told me to run for help, that she'd stay. I ran to the elevator. I pushed "1" and came down. There I saw Carolina and Carrie Ann and we went to the lobby….That's all I know."

"Was the elevator on the same floor when you left Rolanda's room?"

"Yes. I'd just gotten out of it. It was still there when I came back. That's all I know." She began crying until she couldn't talk.

The detective got up and said to Margie, "Do not leave your room. We'll tell you when we want to talk to you. Have your dinner sent up."

The detective nodded to the policewoman after finding out the only thing Carolina had said she did was to help Margie get to the lobby from the first floor and there was a witness.

"Are you going to stay with her?"

"Yes," said Carolina.

Carolina told Margie they were calling her son. Did she want to call him or her doctor or go to the hospital?"

"No, why? I didn't do anything but find her. Please stay with me."

"I'll make arrangements with the dining room to get dinner for both of us."

"I don't want any."

"You may later."

Later, a knock came on the door. It was not the food. The policewoman came back and asked if Margie would give them her clothes. She took pictures first. Margie agreed voluntarily. She went in the bathroom and put on a robe. The policewoman bagged her clothes.

"Good-night. We'll be in touch with you some time later. It's OK to go to bed if you want." She left.

Margie said she wanted to shower. She went to do that while Carolina made tea and waited for the food. It was delivered when Margie came back.

"I want to go to bed. I'll take a pill."

"Have some tea at least."

"Do they think I did it? I just found her."

"How could they?" said Carolina. "They don't know when she died. Should I stay tonight on the couch?"

"No, I'll be OK."

"I fed your cat. I mean I left out food. She seems to be hiding."

"I have to find her. She'll be in the closet if anywhere."

Margie found her.

Before she left, Carolina said, "Call me if you need me. Put the chain on the door and eat the food in the refrigerator if you get hungry."

Carolina left with her own food, going up to her room and avoiding the killing zone. She had to call her friends to tell them she wasn't coming tomorrow and why. She had to take care of

Margie. She thought she should go downstairs to listen if she could learn more but she couldn't. She felt the need to be by herself. She felt disappointed in herself for not preventing this. She had felt something terrible was going to happen. But she couldn't have stopped it. Now her friends were hurt.

Her thoughts on her way to her apartment were troubled: A lot of good my intentions did me—or my friends. I knew something like this was going to happen—and, of course, it had to be Margie who found poor murdered Rolanda. I just hope Margie doesn't start trying to tell those detectives how string theory and sunbursts affect older people and maybe even made one of us kill Rolanda. They'll think she's balmy for sure and think Margie did it. Then they won't be looking too hard at other people. I'll look for other people.

CHAPTER ELEVEN—MARGIE PAYS

Carolina got to her apartment and called her Church friends. She slept. She was awakened by the phone by her bed. She picked it up to hear nothing but she knew someone was on the line. It was unnerving. The number did not show on caller ID. She decided to investigate it later with the phone company. She wondered how the line they had in each room tied into the emergency system panel.

She tried to go back to sleep. She was nervous about Margie, the wanderer, being left alone at night. She'd go down early to see her.

She got up at six and dressed. She went up to Rolanda's area but saw that the room and hall in front of it were taped off but could still be used as an exit in an emergency. There was not much to see.

She did see that the elevator was next to Rolanda's apartment. She ducked under the tape and tested the knobs of the doors of the empty apartments across from and next to Rolanda's apartment with her sweater covering her hand. They were unlocked. She ducked quickly back outside the tape. She hoped there weren't cameras watching. She saw that the emergency door to the stairs could be seen from Rolanda's room if her door was open. It was a straight line from the emergency door to Rolanda's door to the couch, though the couch faced sideways from the door she was told.

Carolina went to Margie's room. She heard a rustling inside. She knocked.

Margie asked who it was and let her in. She was sitting at her table.

"How are you?"

"Awful. Did they say I had to stay in my apartment?"

"I don't think so. Just stay around. They have your cell number. Are you going down to breakfast?"

"Oh, no. I can't face people. They'll all be asking me questions."

"You may be right that it's best not to go down this morning if you're too upset."

"Will you go, Carolina, and see what they're saying?"

"Of course. Is it OK to send our friends up to see you?"

"Only a few. You know my friends."

Carolina thought, *I do? Do you have any?*

"You'll have to come out today or tomorrow or it will look odd. I'll go with you. Come down to dinner tonight or tomorrow," Carolina said.

"I will, unless I'm arrested by then."

"Lots of people could have been there before you. Do you have a lawyer, a good lawyer, to help you if you should need one?"

"No, only someone who made a will for me, not a criminal lawyer."

"We'll see. We'll look for one later on the internet. Do you have something to eat?"

"Cereal. Do you want some?"

"No, I'll have tea. I'll make it for us."

They sat down companionably. Margie ate. Carolina cleaned up.

"I fed the cat," said Margie before Carolina brought it up.

"OK. I'll go. You have my cell number if you need me. I'll be sure to carry it today."

"Thank you, Carolina."

Carolina left thinking how subdued Margie was. Maybe the sleeping pill was affecting her. Or she was holding something back.

She went downstairs to the lobby and the concierge desk. She asked for her mail but there was none. She asked what had happened with the police last night. The concierge said he heard they'd been there a long time interviewing residents and staff and taking pictures. Whatever they do.

"Anyone special?"

"Rolanda's daughter and Miss Dougher."

"Thanks."

Carolina went in to breakfast. She was popular today. All the tables wanted to hear what had happened with Margie.

Carolina sat at the usual one she preferred for breakfast when there were spaces. Lillian, Dot, Joyce and Enid were there. Breakfast was self-service unless one couldn't walk. But even the metal walkers had seats that could be used as trays. Carolina made tea and toast and got some yoghurt. She came back.

"No pancakes today?"

"No, this is enough," Carolina said. She heard them tell her the news.

"They took Rolanda away last night."

"They got the names of everyone around yesterday but most of the people were in their rooms or out of the building."

"Did Margie see anything in the room? We thought she might have done it but they didn't take her away."

"Of course she didn't do it," Carolina said.

Rita said someone claimed they saw Rolanda propping open her door for her daughter. There wasn't anybody else around. It wasn't long after when Gwen heard screaming and went down the hall to see Margie on the floor over Rolanda. Margie got up and ran out to the elevator to get help. "We don't see how she didn't at least see it done," she added tactfully.

"Oh," said Carolina.

"We can't understand why Margie wasn't arrested."

"We bet they're just preparing a case."

Carolina got up to go back to Margie's. Gwen Dougher, who had stayed with the body, was absolutely credible.

What now? thought Carolina, her mind in a dark place.

Annie passed her and asked Carolina to eat with her.

Carolina said, "I need to keep Margie company. She shouldn't be alone. I'll find out when her son is coming in."

"Can I come up?"

"Yes, I think she'd like that."

Annie said, "I think her son is a very young man. I don't know how much he can help. Maybe he can take her away."

"I doubt if she can go."

Annie looked shocked. She said, "We'll have to get her down for dinner. Weren't you going away for the weekend?"

"Not now. Margie is so alone."

"I'll be up later," said Annie.

Carolina went up to Margie's room. She was lying on the couch.

"We have to be prepared, Margie. When is your son coming?"

"I don't know. He said he'd call when he got here, but he asked what can he do? He has to be back in a day for his work."

"Let's look up a lawyer on the internet. If the police come and treat you like a suspect, we must call one. You will not speak unless you are represented. At least that's what they say on those TV police shows." Carolina laughed. "*Matlock* will get you off or *Law & Order*."

Margie laughed.

Margie took Carolina to her computer and they sat on two chairs before it. They retrieved a list of lawyers' names.

"It looks like these lawyers have defended people accused of serious crimes in this area. Type it out, Margie."

"Let's look them up some more to see what kinds of cases they do."

"Do you have money, Margie?"

"Not so much since my husband left me. I didn't ask for alimony. I didn't have a lawyer representing me in the divorce. I thought I'd die within the year. I honestly did. I had to get away from him. He was my husband; I didn't understand how he couldn't understand that or how he could chase women in my face. What if I saw him with someone? It was bad enough to see and talk to them on the phone or the internet. Anyway, I didn't think of putting 'paying for a defense attorney, if accused of murder,' into the divorce agreement. It's too late now."

"Is he out of the picture if you need him?"

"Yes, he's obsessed with other women. I'm nothing but a nuisance to him now. I'm a bug he couldn't squash but had to divorce. I should have told him I liked the schlock paintings he could do in an hour. It was all downhill from there. Did you know the universe is one of many bubbles that are other universes?"

"No, I didn't," said Carolina, "you have to concentrate on what you need now."

Carolina spent the day with Margie. Annie, Rita and Dot came up. It was soon time for dinner.

"Are you going down for dinner, Margie?"

"Can you all eat up here?" Margie asked.

"No, that's not practical," said Carolina. "Come down. We'll be with you. It will be better."

"OK, I'll try."

When dinner time came, they all met on the first floor and escorted Margie into the dining room. Four of them walked Margie to her table. Lillian was out with her family. Carolina hoped they wouldn't sit any stragglers with them who might ask touchy questions and send Margie into tears or admissions or whatever. Margie would be easy to get a false confession from, Carolina thought. She was always ready to confess something. Carolina thought it must have been from her going to that Catholic school she always talked about.

Dinner that night became of infinite importance in trying to make Margie look like she was blending in and had lots of supporters. Escaping life in prison might depend on eating while looking innocent. Chicken Francese with Potato, Eggplant Parmesan or Tilapia Teriyaki with White Rice. They all chose the chicken except for Carolina who chose the Teriyaki, thinking it might be the least unhealthy of the three.

"At least we know what's in most of the dishes. That's good since Lillian isn't here to tell us," said Margie.

The server came out and everything went fast. They were treated like some sort of celebrities. Milton and several other people came over to say hello before they left. Some people seemed to be avoiding them; Rolanda's dining companions were sitting at other tables. Thank heavens none of them had been seated at Margie's table; it would have been like Management to do something like that. Others stared at their table but said nothing. One could hear conversation about "Margie" and "Rolanda" and "arrest" from time to time.

The concierge came in and walked all the way to the back to tell Margie that her son would be there tomorrow morning at ten.

Later, Annie and Carolina sat with Margie in her room.

Margie was saying, "I keep trying to explain these altered states of being to myself: the divorce, this place, Rolanda. I don't use drugs. Prescriptions, I do. Multi-universes, you know. I wish I were in another one."

"Let's watch TV," Annie said.

"Is *The Universe* or, *Through the Wormhole* on?" asked Margie.

Apolonia, the cat, came in and jumped on Carolina. She thought of her own cats she was supposed to be with today.

Annie found an old movie and left it on, tucking the remote in the couch so she wouldn't have to watch those science shows. The new Margie accepted her reality and was quiet.

Carolina got up and said she'd be back after the movie, slipping out the door quietly.

Carolina knocked on Gwen Dougher's door. Gwen answered the door but looked surprised.

"I have some questions to ask you about what you saw yesterday."

Gwen looked reluctant. "I talked to the police. It would be wise to let them handle it."

"The more minds working on the mystery, the more chance it has of being solved," said Carolina.

"I would think you'd mean the 'right' minds. I don't mean to denigrate your intelligence, Carolina, but you are not trained in detection and it might be dangerous. Who knows what will send Margie off?"

"Why Margie? How can you be sure someone didn't get there before her?"

"I saw Rolanda prop open her door; she does that for her daughter who often walks up the stairs there. She leaves the door open and sits on her couch in case she falls asleep, although she wouldn't admit it. She always looked so robust. I heard the elevator stop on this floor by the loud ding. Soon after that, I heard loud screaming and almost immediately I ran out to Rolanda's room to see Margie bending over her. This all happened in a few minutes. I didn't see anyone else. I'm surprised she hasn't been arrested. People shouldn't be left alone with her."

Carolina disagreed with Gwen's conclusion, but left on good terms since the women basically liked each other.

This is not good, thought Carolina, but not as unbelievable as addled Margie being a murderer. Carolina thought that doing things like saving viable worms and putting the injured ones out of their misery showed that Margie was a humane person and not some freak killer.

Carolina went back to Margie's and watched the end of the movie. A knock came and everyone sat unable to move. Finally Carolina got up and answered it. A man in his mid 60s came in and Margie ran up to hug him. "This is my friend, Aaron." The phone rang. "He's already here," she said into it. It was obviously the concierge saying someone was coming up to see her. "Timing and me are awful," said Margie to the group.

Aaron said, "I drove up as soon as I heard what happened. Can I stay here tonight or should I call for a room in a hotel?"

"Is your wife here?"

"She couldn't come."

"I'll try to get you the guest room they have here. Thank heavens you're here. These are my friends, Carolina and Annie. This is Aaron, my friend for over 30 years. He's happily married. We have been through marriages and divorces and the births of our children and everything together. He's the brother I never had."

Annie nodded with a skeptical look but didn't say anything.

Carolina thought it was likely. "Well, Annie and I had better let you get caught up. Remember to call the concierge about that room."

After they left, Carolina said it wouldn't look good for Margie to entertain a married man. She had to be especially careful now. But the friends were glad to be able to go to their apartments.

"That's a handsome man. He looks like an athlete and a scholar. I don't believe he's not her boyfriend sometimes. That's what people do these days, at least in movies I read about in the newspapers," Annie said.

"Give her the benefit of the doubt. Margie doesn't lie, I've noticed."

"Well, sex is a different matter. Lots of people thought it was OK for President Clinton to lie about his exploits. hey thought it was about his personal life and none of anybody's business."

"Margie's son will be here tomorrow or the day after, anyway."

Carolina called Margie later to see if she'd settled Aaron into the guest room for the night. "Did you get the room?"

"No, it was taken. He's going to stay on the couch. We went out since Aaron hadn't eaten yet, and I needed to get out of this place for a while."

"I understand," said Carolina, but added, "The other residents probably won't. You have to be prepared for some unkind remarks."

"People of that generation have dirty minds," said Margie. "I need him here."

"I'll see you tomorrow. Call me if you need me."

A knock came on Carolina's door. A detective wanted to check again on where Carolina had been during the attack and whom she'd seen. Had Mrs. Belbuck said anything to her about the murder?

"Nothing of importance and nothing Margie Belbuck hadn't told the policewoman. She's the most honest person I know. I trust her."

"Did you know Mrs. Belbuck went to Mrs. Rolanda Wolfe's room to ask her why she'd removed her from a dining table?"

"No," said Carolina, hiding her shock from the police. She was appalled but not surprised that Margie had admitted a motive. She was sure the real killer wouldn't be doing that.

The policeman left. She supposed the police were questioning everyone in the whole building.

Margie was occupied the next day by her friend that she had not seen for some time.

Carolina caught up on a lot of her own affairs that day and went to the library before dinner to see what she could learn from the regulars about what had gone on during the investigation. Many people who were passing by came up to Carolina since they wanted information they could pass along to others. Carolina was relieved when dinner time came around since her table group didn't know very much.

Carolina got to her table and saw that everyone was there who should be except Margie. Florence, from another part of the room, was seated in Margie's chair, since many of her dining companions had not shown up and had been spread like seeds among more fertile tables. Management had consolidated tables, one more tablecloth saved for humanity. *Excuse me,* Carolina thought, *I forgot they did that for social reasons to prevent loneliness among the elderly, as they assured us in a meeting they had called once about the dining facilities.* (Carolina felt she must watch a tendency to become cynical; she must just be hungry or very upset about Margie.)

"They say a young man is staying with Margie," said Florence, the guest.

Ike stopped by the table. "I saw Margie leave in a car with a thin man. Is she making a getaway?"

Carolina said he was an old friend here to give her support.

"Is that what they call it these days?"

"Certainly not!" said Carolina.

The dining guest had memory problems. "Margie's son is here?"

"No, her friend."

They ordered. Two got the Lamb Flamade over white rice. The others ordered the Linguine with Clam Sauce and Garlic Bread. They all got clam chowder first. (Clams with clams, what a novel menu.)

Florence asked, "What is 'Flamade?'"

"Shhh!" The rest warned. "We'll never eat if you ask the server."

There was no more talk about Margie. Either the people at the table knew everything or disapproved of her scandalous behavior.

Rita talked about another retirement home she'd visited. "They allowed aides in the dining room there."

Florence replied, "Oh, yes AIDS. Lots of teenagers fall into that trap." It seemed Flo had hearing problems too, like many of the residents.

Not wanting to embarrass Florence, Carolina changed the subject

Florence said, "They say my hearing is slowing down but I hear fine."

"Good," everyone said, with eyes rolling.

Dinner came.

Movies were under discussion. Rita said she liked Mae West.

"She was racy," Carolina said.

Being a fan of Mae West, Florence said, "Mae West was racist? I don't think so." But she forgot about it quickly so clarification was not called for. She apparently had memory as well as hearing problems, but she seemed blissfully unaware of either. She was the opposite of poor Margie who recognized all of her many losses.

Dinner was soon over. They made their way out to the lobby. Margie was there now getting her mail. She and her companion hadn't been out long to dinner. Carolina and Annie went up to her.

Margie said, "I have to get my messages," looking around at the people staring at her and her guest. She said, "I think I'll call from now on."

Carolina stepped away to talk to Aaron while Margie and Annie were talking. Suddenly Ike showed up behind Annie and Margie. He had oyster crackers he had gotten with clam chowder in each hand. He said, "I have a gift for you." He handed a package of them to Annie. Margie put her hand out and said, "Where are mine?" He walked off, seeming not to have heard her. Annie said, "Take these." Margie said with disappointment, "No, I don't want yours, but really. What did Ike mean by that?"

Then Florence, the guest from dinner, came over saying she could see Margie in her son's face.

"He happens to be older than I am. He's a friend," Margie said.

Beverly came up and introduced herself to Aaron. "Where are you staying?"

He told her, "I'm staying on the couch in Margie's apartment."

Beverly took a few steps away and said to someone standing there, "What is a nice looking boy like that doing with Margie? He dresses so nice too. Look at that dark green jacket. He just got his hair cut too. He should show Margie how to dress, but like a girl, of course. But she must know how to do something great that doesn't involve clothes."

Margie suddenly realized she would never live down her reputation, not only as a murderer but now as a sex maniac. Could things get worse?

Margie said good-bye and led Aaron to the elevator. Peace descended on her for the night. She spent a lot of time hearing how Aaron loved his wife and listening to him talking to his wife on his cell phone, although he politely used it in the next room. (Why can't the other residents hear this?) She was happy for him, just realizing what she was missing, a better version of her own husband. Aaron came out to tell Margie his plan to leave next morning to go home since Margie's son would be here by then or soon after.

In fact, he did leave as planned and Margie waited for her son, glad her friends and her son were rallying around her. She would be all right now, she told herself.

A notice went up in the lobby about the funeral the next day. The Home would send a staff member. Apparently, Rolanda was not that well liked by residents (including Carolina if truth be told) since no one else had signed up to go. Rolanda's best friend signed but would drive herself. Carolina didn't think she would learn much there and decided not to go. The sign-up sheet count remained at one.

The concierge called Margie. Her son had arrived. Margie met him at the central elevator on her floor, avoiding the first floor. He said he had rented a car. They went to her apartment.

"How long can you stay?"

"I have to go back tomorrow."

"Tomorrow?" Margie was thunderstruck. "You can't."

He said, "I'll lose my whole time at this internship that might lead to a job. Do you really want that?"

"No, of course not."

"You look OK."

"I have to get out of here."

"You have a lease, Mother. You can't just leave. You didn't hurt anybody. I don't even have an apartment of my own."

There was a knock on the door. This time the door opened to show two police officers.

"Marjorie Lorraine Belbuck. You're under arrest…." Now her son was dumbstruck. Carolina, who'd followed the police upstairs, told Margie they would get her a lawyer. "Don't say anything" (knowing that was impossible). "Lawyer-up."

"Where are you taking her?" demanded her son.

They told him, "To the police department for questioning first. You can follow us."

Margie packed some things and asked Carolina to take her cat. She was taken away in cuffs. Carolina and Margie's son followed her to the police car while everyone in the lobby watched.

"Stand tall, Margie!" someone yelled through the open door. Margie thought it was Milton.

"I'll follow," said her son.

"No," said Carolina. "Your mother and I made a list of lawyers to call. Get a lawyer immediately."

"I have a friend who's a lawyer in New York. He can't practice here, but he should know one who's good. I can't believe this."

Carolina went with him to Margie's apartment. After making some phone calls, he left to meet a lawyer.

She said aloud to no one, "I must find out what happened for Margie's sake. I couldn't save Rolanda but I will try to save Margie, God willing."

Carolina found the cat she had to fish out of the closet. She took it to her own apartment along with cat food and cat dishes. She saw Margie's keys and took them so she could get in later if necessary. She left a sticky note on the door for Margie's son.

"It's OK, Apolonia. Your adopted mother will be home soon. I have a clothes closet for you to hide in."

Margie's son Jesse came back later that day. He said the lawyer had been with his mother. She might not get bail. Jesse had the next day off but had to get back or lose months of work. "Will you help my mother?"

"I'll try. We both know she didn't do it. Did you eat?"

"Yes. Here are the numbers for my Mother, the lawyer and places where you can reach me. I'll go tomorrow to see her and then go back. I'll be in touch when I can be of help. Do you have the keys?"

"Yes, here they are. Will you leave them with me tomorrow? They'll be here for you or her whenever."

"I will." He left.

CHAPTER TWELVE—DINNER COMPANIONS AD INFINITUM

Margie did not get out of jail the next day. Carolina talked to her on the phone.

Margie said, "You remember when you were young and in love and were loved? I was always in pain then because I was afraid there would come a time when I wasn't either of them, when I would be alone. And now it's here. I don't have to be afraid of THAT anymore." She snorted in a despairing way.

Carolina assured her she wasn't alone, but her heart broke. Was she wearing an orange jump suit? Did she have a cell mate? Carolina spent her days thinking of whom to talk to so she could help Margie.

The vacuum created by Margie's absence at dinners was filled with new people every few days.

One woman—Joan—ate there a few days before moving to a table that suited her better. She was a mother of three who had had a large house with a pool near the ocean and who had volunteered as required to fit into her social set. She had loved to go to Broadway to see musicals for years, and her husband had accompanied her to them. She said she had hated the movie version of *Annie Get Your Gun* that had been shown at the Courte recently because she didn't like the horses in it. She saw it on Broadway with Ethel Merman and there weren't any horses on the stage, she said approvingly. Maybe just two at the end. Carolina reminded her of *Oklahoma!*, a movie to be shown in the video room next day—it was musicals week at the home—but warned her there were horses in it.

Joan got her jewelry from Lord & Taylor or Tiffany's, gifts from her parents and then her husband. Her clothes were of excellent quality, the ones from Lord & Taylor, at least. She innocently bemoaned the quality of cashmere these days, even at L&T. It was hard to believe Joan was not a snob, but she wasn't. She was mild and not a bully. Maybe she was a little bit of a snob, but it was part of her culture that she didn't question, not a choice. Joan was not a seeker of truth and would never go out into the desert to find herself. It was safe to say Joan was not a genius.

Most of the regular diners at the table were sorry to see her go—but Joan did not like to be associated with a table that associated with Margie. Carolina thought she might not like having to associate with Lillian every day too, the usual reason for defections.

Lillian continued to interject, "This is NOT food!" every so often during dinner.

Dot wore her hats—a chic cloche navy number one day and a fine Jackie Kennedy pillbox another.

Rita had actually almost stopped leaving her stuff in the trash rooms at night, she was afraid of what walked the corridors. She left some stuff there in the day but was quite improving. She took someone's suggestion to buy one thing a day and to discard one thing. She had an eye on Ike whose girlfriend was being moved to another state by her family. Maybe they were worried about her reputation, or she needed more care or they were afraid of violence in the corridors when she visited Ike. Other people had actually moved out.

Annie asked if Rita had gotten any oyster crackers lately. Rita looked puzzled.

Ira sat with them a few days when he had to come back from Florida to take care of some things, he said, like giving his children some antique furniture now moved from storage to his temporary apartment. He was back for a while, eating at a temporary table. He was staying in the model apartment Margie had been in. Even though he was in his 90s with a cane, he had an excellent mind. Ira's favorite topic was politics and the economy. He said the President could prevent default by using the 14th Amendment like Truman did. He said he had voted for a Socialist candidate, Norman Thomas, once, did we remember him? No one was politically savvy enough for him, and he couldn't stand the multiple proclamations of, "This is NOT food!" either.

Carolina was sorry to see him go, although he changed tables even before he left again for good.

Carolina remembered Margie's conversation with him once in the library. Margie was talking to Ira and seemed to react with discomfort to his disappointment in his companions in this place, well hidden though it was by so polite a man. Margie could be quite intuitive and tried to please. She had tried to think of something intellectual to interest him.

Margie had said, "I was thinking about the difference between Art Deco and Art Nouveau the other night and think I prefer Deco. What do you think?"

Ira had said, "I have no idea, although I'm sure I'm old enough to have lived through both of them."

"Actually, Art Nouveau lasted until WWI. Art Deco was part of the Jazz Age like the Chrysler Building, I think. Its forms were more geometric. I forget." Margie had looked confused. "They were all about design anyway."

Carolina tried to remember the difference between Art Deco and Art Nouveau herself and was confused, like remembering the different kinds of Greek columns.

Carolina's tablemates were trying to get her attention from her reverie. Her tablemates kept asking Carolina about Margie's cat. "She's fine, except during thunderstorms. She's terrified then."

One woman, Daisy, who stayed about two weeks, told the table about a cat she'd once had.

Her old cat ate chicken but only kosher chicken. And the cat knew when it wasn't kosher and wouldn't eat it.

Daisy had a real thing about chicken. She insisted she kept being served chicken no matter what she ordered. She rambled on for a half hour once about how she had ordered veal with tomato sauce and cheese while the rest of the table got chicken. The table agreed they had been served chicken, but she had not gotten the veal they had heard her order. She said, "Why did I get broccoli, since the chicken, not veal, came with broccoli?" The chef came out—not the one in pajamas—and told her she had gotten the veal. He'd cooked it himself. She nodded but said knowingly after he left, "Veal with a WING?"

She talked non-stop but looked blank when asked a question—any question. The table felt relief when she moved, although they all felt personally rejected anyway.

Betty, a frail woman who joined the table, insisted there were coyotes in the nearby park. She was afraid they would attack her dog when she walked it. She now walked with her cane, insisting she would fight them off if necessary. A lot of people were beginning to believe it was dangerous to walk outside because of coyotes and inside because of maniacal killers. Betty hated teachers. She asked if any of her table mates were in that profession. The ones who were denied it. Betty declared, "There are lots of teachers here. My mother was a teacher. She was very mean to me. Teachers cause a lot of trouble. You can tell a teacher by looking at one." She didn't approve of fat people either. It was good Margie wasn't here. (Or maybe not.) Betty became very ill and left for rehab the day after she had told them about teachers. They all missed her.

Before she had gotten worse and left the next day, Carolina tried to talk to her to get details about the dog feud. She also gently tried to talk to her to find out more about a remark Carolina remembered Betty had made about someone knowing Rolanda before she had come here. Carolina recognized that Betty needed specialized medical care and insisted that the home call her daughter or an ambulance. It was too late to get any sensical information from Betty unless she improved. And it was no use after she came back from rehab, much changed in personality, always smiling. She had lost her caustic quality. She couldn't, or maybe she just wouldn't, talk about anything negative.

The next person who came to the table was Phyllis, who almost made Lillian leave. At first, Lillian thought she had found her soul mate when Phyllis yelled at the server: "Bring salads and our drinks NOW! And bring seltzer, tomato juice, coke and coffee for Lillian, I mean Mrs. Katzberg, too." (She had heard Lillian order and not get them.) Then the entrées came and they were not hot enough. Phyllis felt her food with the palms of her hands and Carolina's food too. She insisted they both be taken back and warmed. They came back still not hot enough. She demanded that the chef come out. She told him, "This is NOT acceptable. Some things are acceptable and this is NOT!" Phyllis ordered three different potatoes until she got one hot enough for her. She also took her knife and banged her glass when the server was not fast enough. This got the attention of half of the dining room and embarrassed even Lillian.

Phyllis asked for Carolina's chair one night and got it, Carolina being off-balance that night. She took Annie's chair another night when Annie was late. Carolina and Annie had a meeting about it and decided to fight for their locations. They tried the strategy of coming down early several days but that got old. Finally, the table told her that they had all had their chairs first. She could have one of theirs when one of them moved. And hers was Margie's seat when she came back. It turned out Phyllis was actually a nice person who apologized for her behavior. (Fighting for one's place never ends, like everyone here knew or would find out.) She brought baked goods for them. She liked them. They liked her. Except for the night she sent the table's rolls back as not fresh enough but grabbed one for herself as the basket was being taken away. They never got the basket back from the server that night, probably to spite Phyllis.

Phyllis said she needed more activities. She'd been to Arts and Crafts when she first came here. She was questioned when she got there by the Arts and Crafts group as to whether she was a resident or not. (The other residents really wanted to play word games instead of doing Arts and Crafts.) They wouldn't stop the game they were playing on time, and the teacher let them go on. Phyllis asked, "What about Arts and Crafts?" Phyllis insisted they stay on the written schedule of activities. The teacher finally said that the ladies had to stop their game. They were livid. The teacher said the activity that day was making New Year's Decorations. (It was February.) Phyllis said, "I don't want to do that." The ladies gleefully shouted, "Can we play our games now?" as they watched Phyllis walk away. The last time she went, they were making snowflakes for the windows. She said they were using those blunted scissors like in second grade, much as she had suspected. As she left, she muttered loud enough for the teacher to hear, "I guess I won't miss making Valentines in March!"

One day, Phyllis tried to send back Carolina's plate but this time Carolina fought for it. Four hands pulled on her plate but Carolina won. After that, she didn't want to eat the food. But Phyllis was basically good at the core. The people at the table felt that about the people who came, or the people left. A lot left as soon as they could, even some who were very good people.

Carolina talked to Margie or her son every day. It was hard for Margie. It seemed only she could have done the murder but Carolina knew she didn't.

One night, Carolina and Annie were eating alone at their table. Someone hadn't called about not coming down to dinner or the two would have been transferred to another table, for violating the rule of wasting a tablecloth. They intended to enjoy their privacy that night. Then came dinner. Carolina couldn't eat very spicy food but Annie ordered the retirement home version of fajitas. They had a new cook, and fajitas had never been on the menu before. It came with sauce on the side which Annie poured on her food, all if it. Next thing, Annie turned purple. Carolina gave her all of the water in the glasses on the table. (It must have been Lillian who hadn't called since Carolina gave Annie a seltzer, coke and cold coffee too, not the tomato juice.) Annie lost her voice and couldn't talk through most of dinner, which she went back to eating. Annie claimed never to have eaten Mexican food before, but she liked it. It was lucky that cook left, since Annie lost her voice every time fajitas or other Mexican dishes were on the menu.

CHAPTER THIRTEEN—CAROLINA LISTENS

Carolina and Annie decided to spend some time in the library after emerging from dinner one night. Carolina thought she might hear something of value to Margie if she listened to people long enough. She felt that this situation with Margie was all so wrong—very wrong.

Floyd was playing the piano before second seating. This was the last time before he left for Florida. Women crowded around him in the entertainment room. He had a big following that night. He was playing mostly upbeat songs. Floyd banged out "It's a Grand Old Flag." He knew his audience; most of these people had done something for the country in WWII.

One very loud woman in a walker started to march as she sang the song and got several women, some in walkers, to follow her. She shouted to them, "We should go out and entertain!"

"Where?" someone asked.

She yelled, "To the old people!" She was serious. No one laughed.

Later Carolina asked Annie if she thought that was funny. Annie didn't understand. Carolina said about her saying we should go out and entertain the old people.

Annie still didn't understand. "Oh, she thought we should go sing at some Old Folks Home."

Carolina didn't know what to say. Despite their being in their 80s or 90s, they just didn't think of themselves as old. Margie had thought we were so brave here, but maybe we aren't brave at all, just deluded.

In the library that evening, people came and went, including those who had come back from their outings. They seemed restless, Carolina thought. A group of about six or so collected in a circle around Annie and Carolina.

Daisy said, "I'm missing my necklace. I didn't notice it since I got that emergency pendant for around my neck and I haven't been wearing the ruby one anymore. I have to tell my daughter."

"I wear my emergency pendant around my wrist—the new ones the home has," Lillian said.

Talk developed about the benefits of each.

"They got better when they got smaller," said Annie. Then, "If anybody has found a big yellow sponge lately, it's mine."

People laughed.

Rosemary said that Angie had told her they don't do background checks on possible residents here—financial check yes, but not criminal. We could be living next to Jack the Ripper and not know it. Everyone was shocked.

"They should at least do them on the men," Dot said.

Carolina wondered aloud how much they looked into the backgrounds of the workers who had full access to every area.

Enid said, "If Rolanda had her door locked and her security chain on, she would probably be with us today."

The tone of the conversation was getting gloomy so Carolina asked if any other people were moving. She added, "I heard the Teflon curtains are up around the elevator walls again. Someone is coming or going."

Joyce said they sometimes kept those blankets up for days. There are permanent hooks in the top of the elevator on the wall to hang them on. The janitor was too lazy to take the blankets down, though it seemed easy enough to do.

Shirley came in. She asked why the blankets were still up in the back elevator.

"Ira moved to Florida permanently this time," Enid said. "He said there wasn't enough intellectual activity here. He said they teach courses in some places."

"How can he say that? We have Arts and Crafts and playreading sometimes. I hear Miguel is going to teach Spanish someday too," said Shirley.

"Yeah, it's lucky when eight of us come down to read plays and Miguel will probably get about five people for his class. I don't think that adds a lot to the intellectual meter in this place—maybe 20 degrees."

Shirley said she heard everyone liked the singer the other day. There was an enthusiastic response.

"He tap danced and sang. He brought his own wooden floor. Let's get a lot of people to ask for him again. Did you like him, Carolina?"

"I wasn't there. I heard him practicing 'Honolulu Baby' before the performance on my way past and decided to miss it."

"You missed a good one. I like 'Honolulu Baby.'"

"And we have cable TV," said Rosemary, thinking of what Ira had said. "I like game shows."

"I like *American Idol* and *The Bachelor*," Annie said

Phyllis said, "I would never demean myself by watching reality shows."

Carolina came to Annie's defense. "I like the dance competitions like *So You Think You Can Dance* with young people. They seem to fly across the floor, defying gravity."

Phyllis sniffed in a superior way.

"They have to take those astronomy shows off the air. Maybe they're what drove Margie to do what she did. She was always talking crazy," Rosemary said.

Rita came to Margie's defense before Carolina could. "Maybe you could learn something from them."

There was a shocked silence.

Carolina said quickly, "See, we all learn here. Ira was wrong."

Almost everyone laughed.

Rosemary said: "I can't stand that Freddie. My heating was making popping noises. He said he had been there four times when I wasn't there, and he didn't hear it. But I had three people in there who heard it and told Management about it. And I'm almost always home. I don't believe he was there four times in two days like he said. It took him five minutes to fix it when they made him come. He came with two other workers, Tabor and Reyes, who are better workers. They took something rolling around in the air duct attached to the furnace out. It looked like a plastic bottle to me. Freddie said nothing was there, but the noise stopped. He just won't admit any resident is right. He claimed it was nothing but my imagination. Does he want to be tipped?"

"You know we aren't supposed to tip except during the holidays when they take up a collection," Enid said.

Joyce said, "I talked to Ike when he was with the men and they said, 'Tip! How else are you going to get service? Most women don't know that.'"

Carolina remembered having seen Freddie carrying out a basket of clothes from an empty apartment near the back elevator. "Maybe that's how he's spending his time, doing his laundry."

"He makes trouble so he doesn't have to do anything," Lillian said in her quarrelsome voice.

"He just got divorced. The concierge told me. I hear he and Nadia are an item now. A server told me," said Enid, who was a know-it-all sort of person.

"Does anyone hear a sound like a flying saucer around here sometimes?" asked Florence.

"No, maybe you should get your hearing aid adjusted," said Enid.

"I'm glad those reporters are gone. It was fun to see the Manager on TV trying to explain away a murder. He sounded like he was doing a commercial, going on about the magnificence of the place and how safe it is."

They laughed.

"It was fun to see some of us on TV news."

"I got tired of using the back entrance to avoid them."

"Have you noticed that there don't seem to be any crank calls since some of the people moved?"

"I think it was kids," said Annie. Then, "Margie is writing a book."

"Tell her to put vampires in it," giggled Lillian.

"And zombies," said Annie. "People will buy anything with vampires and zombies in it."

Carolina wondered how they knew that.

Carolina and Annie left to go to their apartments. Annie told Carolina in the elevator, "It can't be one of us. We're too old to go around murdering people."

Carolina answered, "I think statistically the percentage of murderers over 60 is not large."

"How about Ira thinking we were not so smart?"

Carolina was miffed at that herself but said, "He had special interests."

They said goodnight. Carolina had that long walk down two halls when she got to her floor. She was scared these nights doing that, knowing Margie was not the one that killed anyone. That meant a murderer was on the loose.

She thought of the things said that evening. She knew there were lots of foreign workers here, but she hadn't known how many were on the staff; some must work out of sight. She was thinking of a possible smuggling ring, smuggling workers into the country. She rejected it from what she knew of the Management here. She passed the trash room and automatically looked in to see if Rita was still rehabilitated. That was one less problem. Maybe she always needed a boyfriend to distract her from her obsession. She hoped it wasn't just Ike she wanted.

She was thinking of what Annie had said in the elevator about us being too old to murder people. Carolina thought it could be any of us able to use a knife, the older the likelier. We had less to lose. Sometimes our consciences got weaker too, sometimes stronger. Either one of those happening could lead to murder.

Suddenly she stopped. She saw the door to the apartment across from hers close. It was an unoccupied apartment. She didn't think they would be fixing it up at this time of night. She stopped walking. Should she go on? She had ideas about what could have happened the day of the murder. But how could someone know what she was thinking? She hadn't said anything to anybody about actually knowing anything. Had

Rolanda seen something she shouldn't? Could someone think Carolina was a witness too? We know what happens to witnesses here. Mrs. Boynton came out to dump her garbage so Carolina said, "Hello" and walked as fast as she could to her door and put up the chain inside. She hoped that would be enough since so many people had access to the keys to the apartments, probably a universal key to the doors, although there was that duplicate set of keys to each apartment behind the concierge desk.

Actually, when she thought about it, Margie was in a safer place, considering her wandering ways, although those ways might be over now that she had picked an apartment. Everyone seemed to be getting cured of their obsessions.

CHAPTER FOURTEEN—THE BLACKOUT

Then came the week of the flood. A late season tornado narrowly missed their place, although not other places that were close, but the electricity for the whole area went out in the fierce storm. Carolina woke in the night in the dark, the bathroom light she kept on was out. She was prepared. She felt for her flashlight next to her bed. She had several battery-operated and functioning lights. Welcome morning light came and Carolina went down for breakfast for the companionship and the information.

There was no generator for electricity at the home.   The residents were given a cold continental breakfast. People made do. Carolina sat at a table with Joyce and a new man from the first floor in a wheel chair. They missed the regular hot drinks and hot cereal. The juices were still cold and there was milk. The electricity was gone for most of the city. It was an emergency. There was no telling when the electricity would come back on. (Carolina wondered if the prison had a generator and if the inmates there were comfortable.)

A lot of residents were going home with their children who lived close by. Carolina had an emergency radio and knew the conditions but not the plans of the Management for those left on their hands.

News was out that Management would serve sandwiches and finger food, mostly dry like crackers or from cans. The elevators were out and food would be delivered to rooms. There would be a buffet dinner of a limited menu for those that could get to the dining room that night at four. There was a shortage of staff since many couldn't get to work. In fact, families of the residents had a hard time navigating on the roads without traffic lights and with trees down. People were asked to stay home. Luckily, the weather was not extreme but elderly people have a special need for a stable temperature. The emergency lights worked in the halls and lobby but for only a day or two. Then the place would be pitch black inside and out even in the day, even in the halls. To tell the truth, Carolina was a little afraid of the dark. Fear hit Carolina, reminding her to "Screw your courage to the sticking place." Hopefully, she would not end up like Lady Macbeth, dead. She had to find her cane.

Carolina finished breakfast when Ike came up to her table, and Joyce, sitting next to her, stood up. Ike and Joyce automatically embraced each other and engaged in a long episode of kissing. Carolina felt like she was in some bizarre world. What was happening? She found herself thinking that the hardest part of disasters was adapting to change in one's circumstances and everyday life. One reached for light switches, forgetting they didn't work. One just kept up one's habits, and dealing without light and television was disorienting. It must be worse for those who couldn't manage the steps.

The couple simultaneously parted and acted like nothing had happened. Ike said, "Hello, Carolina" and left. Joyce sat down and said, matter of factly, when she saw how uncomfortable Carolina was, "It was nothing. Lots of men kiss me." Carolina felt like she was in the "Twilight Zone." She thought it had looked spontaneous but this was not VE Day. It was like lightening striking before her, startling. She was not used to men grabbing women not connected to them and kissing them like that in public. In her day, they did not even do it with wives except in private. There were the uninhibited students in the 1960s but she had thought that rather natural at the time, considering the political situation. But, really, old people should behave better. She did believe it meant nothing but some temporary need in each other they met, but the signaling had been so non-verbal. Do we all have a silent way of communicating? Maybe there was something to jealousy being a motive for murder. But Rolanda had never shown an interest in any man here that she knew of. Anyway, Joyce looked like she might enjoy male companionship more than most women and was sending out signals.

Leaving the table, Carolina said good-bye. She wanted to see if Annie was OK in her room and bring her food if she needed it. She made her way to the nearest stairwell and climbed up using the railing. The stairs were deserted.

She knocked on Annie's door and Annie said, "Come in."

"How are you?"

Annie said, "I'm OK. But I don't have matches to light the big candles on my table at night."

Carolina said, "I don't have any but will ask around. Do you think candles will set off the fire alarm?" But then Carolina thought the alarm system must be out. The big alarm system worked via the telephone landline somehow. There were individually operated fire alarms too in the rooms. Carolina had extra battery lights she would bring over. She would get her radio so they could listen to what was happening. She would bring her cell phone so Annie could call her children. "I guess your landline is out too?"

"Yes."

Annie had food in the refrigerator she wanted to use before it went bad. They could have lunch later.

Carolina went for the phone and radio and lights. She had given presents of emergency lights for Christmas last year. The emergency hall lights were dim and far between. It would be pitch black when they all went out. She felt like a sitting duck, then felt foolish for being paranoid. But it wasn't like there wasn't a dead body to think about. She got back to take care of Apolonia and clean her litter and take the trash out as well as to collect other things to take to be comfortable during the day with Annie. She was glad for some company, but the halls were frightening.

Carolina had to make two trips to carry all of this. She arrived at Annie's bearing armfuls of gifts.

"No matches, Annie."

"I'll call my son. He has matches."

Carolina gave her the cell phone and turned on the radio quietly.

After a while, Annie said, "My son has to go to his sick girlfriend and my daughter has to work at the hospital. I'm going to stay here."

"Management has to take care of us. We'll be together," said Carolina. "Thank heavens Margie had lots of cat food. I wonder if the prison has emergency lights".

The day passed companionably. Antigone, from the dining room, knocked on the door, asking if Annie was staying and if she wanted dinner. Carolina told her she herself would go down for dinner, but they might find her here if she was not in her room, if they were ever looking for her. Antigone reminded them that the emergency lights would go out that night and Management was recommending going to their children's houses or somewhere else. Dinner with limited choices was at four in the dining room, and residents who couldn't manage the stairs would get a sandwich sometime in the evening in their rooms.

People kept their doors open to know what was happening. It helped to get air circulating too, although it would get chilly in the night. At quarter to four, Carolina told Annie she would go to dinner alone to see what she could find out. She would see her soon. Carolina welcomed the doors being opened of the people still there. She talked to each person as she passed.

She got down to find the dining room quite crowded for this time of day. Carolina thought more people would have gone to their families. Servers were handing out sandwiches on plastic plates and juice in bottles at a buffet with lots of leftover "fresh" desserts they had probably been hanging on to when there was refrigeration to serve later. One woman, who must have been overcome with the situation, was shouting, "They are treating us like animals! Animals!" She counted on her meals served on nice china at her table.

People sat at any table. They talked about what was happening. Most were leaving the next morning. They talked about the notices they had gotten the previous day about the aides who were to speak only English in the public areas. What was that about? A whole list of things for aide behavior had been distributed before the big blackout. No food must be given to them from the dining room, there must be no participation in activities or entertainment by them, etc.

And they discussed a notice that residents have to go to our own rooms that night, probably to know where they were and to get them out of the way.

Carolina left to go back to Annie's. Annie had received a roast beef sandwich and cookies and a bottle of juice. She had gotten a bottle of water for Carolina.

Then Carolina put a battery generated light in Annie's bathroom. "That will give you light for your bedroom and bathroom if you get up in the night."

"Thank you," Annie said, then added, "Let's listen to music."

People said hello through the open door as they passed by with flashlights on their way to their own rooms.

Annie and Carolina talked, some of it about Margie.

Carolina said, "Remember how we spent New Year's Day? Margie was here but we didn't know her then. We got party hats and a glass of wine at two in the afternoon, and a singer who sang 'Auld Lang Syne' at three. We got two glasses of wine that day if we wanted it."

"They served dinner at four for both seatings so the staff could go home to celebrate."

"Remember that time when we were talking about tomorrow being May 5th and there was going to be a party that day for Cinco de Mayo? Margie asked us if we had to get our Red flags out and we were so shocked, those who knew what she meant." (Communism was not popular among the old set.) "She has a great sense of humor, but most people don't know when she's making a joke, and she doesn't realize it. She knows too much for her own good but seems dense about people. Poor Margie. She should have learned how to make jokes from Milton," said Carolina.

"Margie said she spent Valentine's Day watching from her window while the florists' trucks pulled up all day and unpacked flowers but she knew none of them would be for her. She had a bad year."

"I can't believe the police are ignoring the fact that they can't identify the fingerprints on the knife found in the body. They're saying it's easy to cover the knife handle with anything like clothing. To them the case is tight in every other way."

Suddenly the lights went out in the hall. It was as dark as it gets in these big buildings when the lights go off inside and the pole and flood lights outside too. One is shocked by total darkness. Carolina got up and turned on a flashlight she had brought for Annie that they had been sitting by and said, "I'll go and see if anyone is caught in the dark now. They really should have a uniformed security guard for a place this size. Is that bathroom light I brought enough until I get back?"

"Yes, you go."

She left to hear someone calling in the hall farther down. It was Joan whom Carolina escorted to her dark apartment. Then Carolina went down the stairs nearest to Annie's apartment. The stairs were awful. She told people she met in the dark to wait, gathered them together on each landing and took them to their rooms on each floor. They were frightened, but most old people had been in disasters before and wanted to do their part. Carolina was proud of them. They bemoaned the situation since they wanted to band together but had been told to go to their own rooms.

Carolina was tired. She went back to Annie's apartment. She told Annie to keep the radio. She had another little one in her apartment. Annie said she would go to bed.

"I'll need the flashlight but I'll bring you another light tomorrow. I hope the one in your bathroom holds up. Lock the door when I leave."

Carolina made her way back to her apartment, dodging carts the servers had left in the halls. She saw individuals sitting in their rooms with flashlights, some that had come in the new giftbags Management had given out when they had moved in and signed leases. These apartments with open doors were near the central area. The doors were closed the closer she got to her own apartment. This was a nightmare. The Management knew the emergency lights were going to go out. Why hadn't they given all of the residents flashlights or set something up in the halls with batteries to give out even a little light? They would survive but the conditions were ridiculous for a home for the elderly. She hoped the murderer was stuck somewhere and not able to get to her.

On that note, she got into her apartment. She found her old radio. She got ready for bed—at least they had running water. She took time to fill up pans of water in case they would need it. She left on a little battery light and prayed she had enough batteries for the duration. The city was still without lights, even traffic lights. She fell asleep wondering why the traffic lights didn't have battery back-up.

Carolina woke to dim daylight, grateful for another day and light. She got up, dressed and found her other flashlight she would use for the halls. She would see if she could escort more people today. The stairs and halls were pitch black. She would suggest Management get more flashlights to hand out to people. (They later were to sell some at the concierge desk.) She went down to find only the concierge there with no lights to hand out. He said, "Danish and juice in the dining room. They would be going to the rooms to give them out too. Was she staying?"

"Yes," said Carolina.

There was a feeling of camaraderie in the place. A lot of people were waiting in the library with packed suitcases for their families who would take them away. An ambulance was outside for an invalid who never came out of his room. Ambulances came on and off all day.

The concierge was busy as a crew came in with a stretcher for pick up. The concierge pointed to a stairwell. But there was not enough light for a stranger to see anything but an EXIT sign. The halls were that dark. The EMT in charge said his flashlight wasn't working. Carolina said, "I'll take you." They followed her up the stairs with the little light she had to the second floor. She searched door numbers for the room. She left them there, finding out the patient had a flashlight. She told them to be careful of the carts in the halls.

There wasn't going to be much help today. She made it down to the lobby to find an aide who needed to get to an apartment but couldn't see far. Carolina took her up, amazed at the little light the small windows gave to the stairwells in general.

Carolina helped more people get to the first floor. They didn't have flashlights. She convinced one person that she shouldn't drive to a hotel since they might not have lights either. (It turned out at least one hotel did have a generator.) But the woman shouldn't be driving as advised by the authorities or by anyone's advice who had seen her drive, especially in these conditions.

Carolina went down to the dining room. She found out Lillian and Rita had gone home to family. Ike and some of his poker mates were still there. They were by the window of the card room playing.

Carolina found Paul by the main elevator. He didn't know how to get to his room since the main elevator was out. Carolina had thought he was a confident man with all of his faculties, but it turned out to be because he did the same things every day. He could only operate in certain conditions. He had fooled everyone. He asked where the other elevators were. Carolina said they were all out. He asked if the elevators went to every floor. Carolina said yes but they'd have to walk up. He did not know where his apartment was. He only knew how to get there from the main elevator. He had more than a sight problem. Carolina took him to his floor using the staircase by the main elevator, but he didn't know which way to turn when they got out. He couldn't remember his apartment number as he and Carolina walked back and forth down the halls. He must have passed his apartment several times. He was in good shape from long walks in front of the building, but Carolina was tired. Finally she went door to door looking for names on the door. She found his. He let himself in with his key as Carolina illuminated the key area. He turned back into his old self again, a man in charge of himself. He said good-bye as though she'd just been passing by, but Carolina saw him turn around in the light from his big window and saw a beaming happy face.

Carolina made it back to Annie's place that now had the door opened. She wondered what others things people were hiding like Paul. She spent some time with Annie and left for her own apartment. She petted Apolonia for a while and sat in the armchair in her bedroom near the window. She read. She fell into an exhausted sleep.

Carolina awakened to hear what sounded like the door being knocked down. She was terrified. She got up to see Freddie, who was unlocking her door, booming that "This place is being evacuated and you have only 10 minutes to get to the lobby with a suitcase."

Carolina said, "I can't leave. I have the cat. Can I take her?"

"NO!"

"Then I can't go. I'm OK here."

"It's a police order." He left and Carolina heard him banging on another door.

Carolina felt totally stripped of any dignity and privacy. She panicked.

She put down lots of food and water for Apolonia. She changed the litter and carried the old litter to the trash.

She came back to throw some things into a suitcase. She had to get her medications sorted out, her purse and her flashlight. She realized all of this had taken a long time and feared the buses would leave her here alone. She grabbed a jacket and realized she couldn't carry all of this and her flashlight, so she tucked the flashlight into her purse. She thought she'd walk straight to the stairs most people used near the main elevator. She thought she might meet people on her way. She wanted to stop to see Annie on that floor. Annie would need help getting down. It was darkest black in the halls. She wasn't thinking. Freddie had scared her. It was a big mistake. She walked fast down the hall with her hands and mind full, with her flashlight in her pocketbook. Then BANG! She walked into a wall without protecting herself at all. She hit her face on the wall and was knocked flat on her back. She lay there a long time. Her eyes were open but not seeing anything. She did not know if she was blinded or if the hall was that dark. She felt for her glasses that had been knocked off. She found them and put them on although they did not help in the dark. She got her flashlight out of her purse. She made her way back to her own apartment carefully. Although disoriented, she knew that way back. She had left her jacket on the floor. She got home but knew she must leave. She went in to sit anyway. A person does strange things in a panic in the dark. She felt like the horse heading back to a burning barn that is home. She understood Margie and her strange behavior better. Margie had just lost her home when she came here and was looking for another one, but none of these apartments were home to her. After a while, Carolina stood up and this time went to the nearest stairs. Using her flashlight and leaning on the railing, she went to the first floor and then to the lobby. Her face was banged up and people made way for her, knowing she was injured. She told them she had walked into a wall. She sat down in a chair. The concierge asked her if she needed an ambulance. he did not know if she had a concussion or a broken nose but said no. She needed to come to herself. She had never acted like this in an emergency. She would take her chances. Some women on staff brought her ice in a cloth for her bloody face. They then went on to other things.

Residents formed a circle around her. She saw there were lots of people waiting for the bus. She saw Annie. Others were coming down from upstairs.

She heard they were being bussed to various hotels. Some hotels had generators or had their power back. The police were there to make sure everyone went. Carolina told her friends that she had been told by Freddie that she had had ten minutes to get out.

"Freddie said the same thing to me. I don't pay attention to him. I took my time," Joyce said.

"I was told by Angie that I had an hour to get ready. They collected us and helped us down. They carried some of us, some men that came with them," said Shirley.

Another ambulance was out in the entrance for one of the invalids.

Carolina was asked again by Angie if she wanted to go to the emergency room.

"No, I could sit there all night and not be seen. I need rest."

Staff herded them into one of the buses. Annie was with Carolina. The bus left some residents off at a hotel in walking distance of the Courte but the rest were taken to another. They got off and were shown to the hotel desk. There was a line to register, and they needed their credit cards. They were told to keep their receipts. They went up to their rooms, Carolina and Annie, on the same floor. Annie's daughter met them up there and took Annie to her home. Carolina went to her room. She turned on a light and felt a thrill and thanked God for lights.

She washed her face and lay down and felt the fresh sheets with relief. It was a good room. She almost fell asleep when she remembered something. The wall she had hit back at the home jutted out from the other wall a little. There was a recess, enough for a person to hide in. If one flattened oneself out, one could not be seen from some angles by someone looking down the hall. That explained it. She thought she had known who, but had thought it was impossible because of witnesses not seeing her. She had known it wasn't Margie, but it had seemed like it had to be. It wasn't.

Carolina got up excited. She would call Room Service for dinner. She ate and thought about how to proceed. She had gotten her reason back. How could she prove who did the murder? She couldn't.

She was exhausted; she would think about it tomorrow. (At times we are all Southern Belles.)

The next day, most of the people made it back to the old homestead. Lights were on, the elevators worked. There would be hot food for dinner.

People from the other bus, and those coming from their children's homes, commiserated with Carolina about her bruised face. "Yes, the swelling is going down, and I don't have a concussion because I feel fine."

She had a satisfying reunion with Apolonia who surprisingly was not in hiding in the closet. Canned food was happily consumed and the cat reassured; it would be hard to give up this cat when Margie got home, as Carolina would try to

Grochmal 155

insure with a little help and before there could be
a trial.

She emptied her spoiled refrigerator, saving
only a few condiments. She still had peanut butter
and bread with some canned soup. She wondered
when she could order groceries to be delivered
again. She had lunches to buy for that was not
provided by the home, and she liked to breakfast
in her own apartment, and she needed cat food
and litter. Maybe tomorrow she could order for
those needs.

She took out the trash with the spoiled food.

Everyone was so relieved to be back and to
have a working elevator. The people on the first
floor gloated a lot to the others about having
insisted on a first floor apartment even though
they were noisy. The "Penthouse" residents were
properly chastened. Rivalry began again.
Carolina had always considered it innocent and
hoped it still was.

When she got back this time, she put the chain
up even in the day, otherwise one might as well
leave the door wide open with all of those keys
around that people had access to. There came a
time when she even put a chair under the door
knob.

CHAPTER FIFTEEN—CAROLINA PRODUCES PEACE AND ORDER

Carolina met people in the lobby and library who had come back, socializing and sharing their experiences of the "flood of the decade." Carolina was speaking out about how Management should have had battery lights bought and hung in the halls after the lights went out and evacuation training for the staff and an organized removal made to the lobby, floor by floor.

Someone added, "And flashlights for the people who didn't have them and for visitors when they came in. Management, wherever they were, didn't care about us here at all."

"Some staff did. They made extraordinary efforts to get here and we know who they are."

Lillian said her granddaughter had put on jeans and sneakers and put her (expensively coiffed) hair in a ponytail and waited on them all by candlelight in their house, even taking care of the dog. She told her grandmother she might become a nurse. (Carolina was sorry for the clone jokes the OTHERS had made. Seriously, she was thankful for seeing again what spirit of giving can bloom in the unlikeliest young people. She had forgotten for a while without knowing it.)

They filed into the dining room. Carolina saw with relief that her group was there with an empty place saved for Margie.

Carolina sat in her seat with Annie next to her, and Dot wearing a fetching forest green bucket hat, and Lillian eager to give her opinions about the food, and Rita with seemingly no problems at all unless her heart was pining for someone other than Ike whom even she realized was taken.

They exchanged stories about what had happened to them in the evacuation. Their favorite server came over asking if they wanted drinks and bringing a tray with seltzer, tomato juice, coke and coffee on it for Lillian.

They looked at the menu: Sweet and Sour Chicken (in batter) with white rice, Meatloaf with gravy and mashed potatoes, Sole Piccata with potato pancakes.

Everything came hot and together for each of the diners. The corn chowder was good, the house salad ordinary. Lillian didn't say a word.

Then Carolina said she needed their help. They listened with anticipation. Not many people needed their help anymore, except with a check.

"I know who killed Rolanda. I don't know how to prove it. I need to flush the killer out. I need you to spread the word that I know who did it but don't say who. I will tell people and staff too. Like I said, tell them I didn't tell you who, remember to say that. Then I need to be with you maybe even at night since I might not be safe. There really is safety in numbers in this case. The murderer killed to maintain anonymity and will not do anything in front of a witness. I will tell you for your safety to think about it. If you are reluctant, tell me. I believe you will all be safe if we take precautions."

"Tell us. Tell us what you want us to do."

"You've had faith in Margie; I'm asking you to have faith in me. Keep your doors locked with the chain up and don't take your trash out alone. I'll make a call to authorities asking for a certain person to be watched, and the danger should be over in a few days."

They began that very night talking to their server, to the concierge and to everyone in the library.

Carolina made a strategic call to the woman detective who protested their behavior and said they already had the killer. That's probably why she didn't insist they stop.

"Come over and I'll show you how it was done," said Carolina.

Carolina stayed nights with her friends. She took a few chances going to feed Apolonia and going home after escorting her friends here and there.

She encouraged Margie that all would be over soon. She hoped. She got a lot closer with her friends.

One day, as they all sat in the library with some other people, conversation broke out as it does. One person lamented the early departure of Floyd to Florida, and another the bug bites she was getting inside the building from invisible bugs while she showed them her welts. They spoke about promises from the Head Chef of a new healthier menu with terms explained. And they mentioned Nadia was not showing up—the concierge said she'd just stopped coming since the flood. And no residents would be allowed behind the concierge desk anymore, even to get their papers. They talked about the edicts Management had passed regarding the aides.

Carolina thought there would be enough time to sort out the aides' predicaments later. Instead, she smiled. Tonight would be a good dinner, whatever they served.

They went in to dinner. Five as usual. Carolina told the Manager that they all wanted that last chair ready for Margie. They were patronized for a while. Margie had better show up soon.

When entrees were served and there was a time of quiet, Carolina began:

"I knew who did it, you know, when I figured out why certain things began to go missing—trinkets and then more valuable things. That was to confuse people, to make the old residents seem unreliable, mislaying their things. But the big yellow sponge of Annie's was the most interesting thing taken. I believed these things were taken. Some were put back in odd places. The staff, the families, the police didn't trust our memories, but I did. Take Annie's sponge. She knew something was wrong when it was replaced with a different one. Nadia wanted a big sponge she could cut into to put things in when she stole them, like that single earring. The sponge would be a fast place to conceal things and seemed normal for her to carry. She was in your apartment, Annie, when she slipped your ring from the drawer in it when you came into the room. Did you ever miss it? She took the sponge and returned another sponge she bought of the same color. It was not quite the same and smaller, but she thought you'd never notice, being so old.

We don't often miss things until we go looking for them, and we're rather careless of our good things. Things don't mean so much to us anymore except the things that are so precious that we keep them on or close to us. We've given most of it away to our children who've put it in a "safe" place. Anyway, Nadia liked the yellow sponge and kept it on her cart when she was working. You saw it, Annie, and wondered what was wrong with the cart, but you got distracted by me and Dot and then Angie showing up with the police.

I don't know how, but Rolanda caught on to what Nadia was doing. She saw her take something or go into someone's apartment not on that person's cleaning day. Maybe something fell out of the sponge. She was going to report her. Nadia must have seen somehow that Rolanda knew and then was told by the concierge not to clean Rolanda's apartment that day. Nadia had to stop Rolanda from telling. She took a chance. Wearing a scrub glove, she got a knife from an empty apartment with household things in it so it wouldn't be identified but that had prints on it that would confuse the police. She went up to

Rolanda's room by the stairs to see her door open. She took the chance that Rolanda had not told anything to the police, waiting to tell her family. Actually, Rolanda was on the couch waiting to tell her daughter. She had no idea Nadia knew she knew. She felt safe. Nadia walked in and stabbed Rolanda. When she heard the elevator stop, Nadia hid in the kitchen area behind the counter that divides the kitchen from the living room. Then Margie got off the elevator and got to Rolanda just in time to hear Rolanda's last breath. Nadia ran out in the mere seconds it took for Margie to bend over Rolanda. She was afraid the big fire door would make lots of noise if she opened it right behind Margie who could turn around and see her, so she headed the other way but heard a door open farther along the corridor as Margie was screaming for help. Gwen Dougher looked out but did not see Nadia, who had pushed the elevator that was still on her floor to "open." There was an indentation in the wall by the elevator and Nadia pressed herself against this and couldn't be seen by Gwen from her doorway. In the confusion and screaming and people calling, she slipped in the elevator door as it opened. Gwen came down the hall but Nadia was in the elevator, the door just closed. Gwen sent Margie for help and Margie ran for the elevator. Nadia slipped behind the blankets hanging on the walls from when Ira had moved. They were black. She was waiting for a moment to start the elevator but Margie was there by then pushing the open button. So Nadia was in one of the corners where the blankets met each other and were not flush with the walls. Margie was too hysterical to notice. Nadia's black shoes did not show beneath the black blankets and the wall was mahogany brown. Margie would later swear the elevator was empty— —she was a witness against herself. Margie got to the first floor and got off where I saw her running down the hall and fall. Carrie Ann and I picked her up and were taking her to the lobby. Nadia held the elevator door open after Margie left and just had time enough to run into a vacant apartment whose door was unlocked next to the elevator when Shirley and her friends were coming in, asking us what was the matter. We said we didn't need help and they proceeded to the elevator which was on the first floor as Margie had left it. Everyone swore nobody had been in the hall after Margie had gotten off the elevator and Shirley got on. After we turned the corner, Nadia slipped out the exit door and acted like she was coming from her car to work, walking down the sidewalk to the central entrance. She acted as surprised as everyone else at Margie's report. It all depended on luck and timing for Nadia. Nadia was clever too, at least at criminal activities (though not as clever as she thought). She had probably even turned her black apron around in the empty apartment to hide any blood splatter that might have been on her dark clothes. With her quick wits and speed, Nadia could have been a great cat burglar if she would have learned alarm systems and had a bit more savoir faire. She underestimated her opponents, however. The murder looked like it could have been done by no one but Margie from the witnesses who thought they'd seen everything but were distracted by the noise and the illusion of a straight hall. Even Shirley and her friends coming in from outside thought they could see right down the hall to Carolina, but their vision on the end was just a bit obscured by the door frame in case Nadia was a few seconds short of getting into the apartment.

It came to me when I hit that wall during the evacuation.

They'll believe me now. I couldn't prove any of it, so I thought flight from the law would be the best proof, enough to get Margie out of jail, anyway. They'll investigate and find jewelry or the things Nadia stole. They wouldn't look when they thought Margie had done it.

We're safe now. We were in danger like Rolanda if Nadia continued to steal. She will say if anyone else is involved. Thank heavens she didn't try to repeat her efforts to silence anyone else. I think the flood prevented it, since cleaners were not supposed to be here, but she could have come on her own. (She might have been here, thought Carolina, but wouldn't scare the others with her unsettling experiences.) Nadia must have thought her game was up when someone called telling her of rumors about what some of the residents were saying about knowing who had done the murder, and she thought she should get out. But they would have suspected her too if I had been body number two, since I had alerted the police about Nadia. Either way, Margie would be freed. But I took precautions, thanks to you. Thank you, my dear friends.

By the way, the fire alarms were co-incidences, water leaks from the ceiling going through the walls to the alarms even on the 3rd floor."

"We heard," they said all said.

"You forgot to explain why my brand of detergent got switched," said Annie.

Carolina avoided answering that question that had involved a real lapse of memory on Annie's part by asking Lillian how the food was today.

And it happened that Margie was released in a few days' time. (It was odd how much more they loved Margie while she was gone.) Margie swore eternal gratitude to Carolina and her friends who had delivered her from prison.

She was reunited with her cat that moved back in with her, but she said Apolonia was still acting like she saw invisible things, so Margie said she might have to start looking for a new apartment.

Margie hugged all of her dining partners in tears. She had trouble getting near Dot who was wearing a big white Kentucky Derby hat with an enormous brim and far extending curlicues, in celebration.

Margie was eager to tell her dining companions all of the things she had waited to tell them for so long:

"Did you know that Quarks contain 'strange' particles—yes, they are called 'strange'—and can turn the whole earth 'strange,' that is, into some kind of mush?   You don't want to mess with Quarks."

"I forgot to tell you that I once ate at that table behind us on the other side of the room. A man who eats at that table came with a weed he picked from the park near here. He said it was an ancient weed, uh, food, they ate in Europe for hundreds of years, in the Middle Ages even. Would you take the chance and eat it? We all had to, he was watching. He fried it in bread crumbs and we all got some with dinner. It tasted like burned bread crumbs."

And: "The worms near the big building next door are a foot long and really thick like snakes. I saved one today from drying out on the sidewalk when I went to the bank, using a stick I picked up from the ground. I couldn't bear to pick it up with my hands. I wonder if they came with a special topsoil they paid a lot for or if they are doing something odd in that building."

And: "Sir Isaac Newton said the end of the world would be in 2030 but the Mayans said 2012 and we know that didn't happen. Even though we are here after 2012, we won't ever know about 2030. I mean we will probably be dead anyway, you know?"

And: "I saw Ike has a ledge on the front of his apartment and there is a little tree under it. I wonder if I can talk to him about letting me in there if we have a real fire and climbing on that ledge and jumping with Apolonia into that tree to save her…"

And: "In jail no one wanted to eat with me at my table. The Matron said they told her they were afraid after what they had heard I was charged with doing and why. Afraid of me! Isn't that funny? I don't know. Why do you think they didn't want to eat with me?"

Everyone started to roll their eyes and avoided looking at each other. Each was wondering how she could jump tables without getting Margie to follow her.

CHAPTER SIXTEEN—LIFE AFTER PRISON

Life settled down a little bit at the table along with Margie, enough to live with her, for two hours a day maybe. They all were very fond of her, weren't they? Dot stopped wearing her celebratory hat and bought some workaday hats that housewives or clerks would wear to the butcher's shop or to work in the 1950s, Woolworths' gray felt hats with a cheap pigeon feather on the side. Carolina didn't like the mood and hoped for an outrageous fascinator someday or at least a pretty church hat. Carolina really started to worry when Dot wore a black mourning veil one day to dinner.

"Did anyone you know die recently, Dot?" Carolina asked.

"No, why?"

"Well, your hat."

"Don't you like it?"

"No, not much. You have so many. I like the cheerful ones better."

"I wear what feels right."

Carolina looked at her friends, Annie, Dot, Lillian, Rita and Margie. They looked like a gloomy bunch. What had happened to their sense of accomplishment and jubilation at saving Margie?

Rita had given up the idea that she was a hoarder and had turned into one. Stuff was everywhere in her place. (Ike's girlfriend had been taken to another state and things looked sort of hot between him and Joyce. Rita needed a man of some sort in her life. Carolina wondered how long Joyce would be able to pay at the Buckingham. But she looked like she could handle Ike. Carolina didn't know if Rita ever could. Carolina decided she would look around her Church for someone for Rita, since pickings didn't seem good around the Buckingham, and someone had to look out for Rita's money. There were many unscrupulous men even over 80. Carolina would pray about it. It was a shame Rita couldn't get interested in a church of her own. She really needed her children to take her to Paris on a shopping trip, but they were too high powered for that. Rita didn't need a nurse but could use one of those paid "companions" from the nineteenth century, a savvy one who knew the foreign capitals. Rita could use one of those Continental World Tours that rich young men of the nineteenth century used to take before settling down. Maybe Carolina could talk to Rita's children one day. Rita needed a vacation.

Annie continued to be Annie. She went to aerobics with her walker, to the movies and to the "entertainments." Her children came about twice a week to visit. Still, she talked more about "going home," making Carolina worry about her.

Then there was Margie. Margie's sense of liberation had faded. Jail had done something to her. She was edgy even for Margie and kept looking for the police to come for her. Carolina was going to ask for a letter from the police or District Attorney exonerating her as a "person of interest." But maybe the letter itself would scare her, who knew?

Now for Lillian. One night, weeks after Margie had returned, Lillian said she had an announcement to make. The table got quiet. Announcements in these places could be bad news from a doctor. Lillian continued: "My daughter-in-law is retiring and they feel they have more time for me. My granddaughter is not a baby anymore and is quite a big girl now. They want me to live with them. I'm going to try it for awhile to see how it works. I may be back soon. Who knows? I will be back to visit you. I've given notice and will be gone by the end of the week. My furniture will be here for a month or two in case I want to come back. I have to pay for those months anyway until my lease would be up. My granddaughter can't wait, and we're going shopping for the room on the first floor they're getting ready for me. I wonder how my daughter-in-law will manage the food. I know she took cooking classes from some fancy school a long time ago. I have a feeling she may hire a part time cook too. It helps to have children in their 60s when they retire who have money and want to spend it. The food can't be worse than in this place right?"

The other ladies at the table looked sad at the news but happy for Lillian. They didn't say what they were thinking: It should happen to all of us, for our families, if we had any, to decide they just couldn't live without us.

Margie looked the saddest at that thought and the happiest. She wished her husband would have a change of heart but knew he wouldn't.

"Is anything wrong with your apartment, Lillian?" Margie asked.

Lillian looked surprised. "Like what?"

"Noises. Does everything work?"

"No noises. Yes, everything works."

"What about ghosts? Do you hear or see anything funny in the apartment? My cat is still reacting to things she seems to see. She tries to get out the door or else hides in the closet. She won't look out of the window while sitting on her cat condo anymore like she did in the other place. Do you think maybe I can stay in your apartment with Apolonia to see how she reacts?"

"Well, after my furniture is put in storage, I don't care what you do with the place, especially after it passes inspection with Freddie."

Margie looked disappointed. It looked like her wandering ways would continue, looking for Shangri-La.

After the procession of the walkers, Carolina followed Annie to the elevator. Life was not the same for Annie since Floyd had gone to Florida. Annie asked Carolina if she would come up with her to talk and Carolina agreed.

Annie and Carolina sat in the comfortable living room recliners like in the days of the flood and talked.

"Are you going to the movie later?" asked Carolina.

"No, who do you think requested *Alien vs. Predator 3*?" (Annie usually went to anything, including the slasher films.)

"It makes you long for the days of *Melinda, Melinda*, doesn't it?"

"Or that Smurf movie. Angie has to learn to weed out the requests made as jokes."

"Maybe Angie fills out those forms to get even with us."

They laughed together.

"So will we miss Lillian? Remember how we wished she'd go away when she first came to our table?"

"I got used to her," said Annie. "I'll miss her and that gruff voice of hers, annoyed with everything. Maybe she'll be back."

"Now when people move from our table, we can't keep blaming Lillian for it."

After a pause to show that she did not appreciate that remark, Annie added, "Something is still wrong here, isn't it, Carolina? Was that thing with Rolanda all of it? I still feel something."

"I know. I wanted to say something but thought I didn't want to be ungrateful for the danger having stopped from that episode. It's something from one of us at our table, isn't it? That's why we can't get back to normal everyday boredom. I shouldn't have said that. We should be glad when everything is OK. There's enough misery when something bad actually happens. I know that. We're reasonable women. Our families and friends are doing well. Nadia had accomplices but not from here. She'd been trying to recruit a bit, they think, and caused a lot of trouble with the staff, but that's over. It still feels as if something else is just not right."

"So what can we do now?" Annie asked. Her assessments agreed with Carolina's: "I don't remember anything I've actually seen this time. Rita needs a boyfriend, one who travels. Margie needs a quiet apartment, although maybe no place here will suit her well. She could be moving forever or until Management puts their foot down. Too bad her husband wasn't a better man but he doesn't want her home in any case. Dot's hats are not cheerful lately. They haven't been for a long time with some exceptions. I don't like them."

"I don't either, Annie, and I used to look forward to seeing her hats."

"Oh, let me tell you some happy news. One of my granddaughters is getting married, did I tell you?"

"No," said Carolina, "wonderful. To that nice young man who was here a few weeks ago? I like him."

"So do I," said Annie. "We're getting old. When we were young we looked forward to everything, to being great-grandparents even. We didn't realize we would be so old when we were in walkers."

"I know. And I think it might be good that Margie's husband doesn't want her back unless he had a change of spirit. He would hurt her again. I don't trust her judgment of men. She'd pick another womanizer or carpetbagger. It's hard to think they were married for 25 years. She lives with so much drama now. I wonder if she was blind to his behavior. She made it sound like he was suddenly possessed by Bluebeard. Speaking of possessed, Apolonia did not act scared and hiding at all when she was with me. Maybe it's Margie. You didn't have the feeling something was wrong before she came to our table, did you? Of course that feeling could have come to you when Rolanda first hated Margie that much. What could Margie have said to bring that on?"

"It could have just been Margie being Margie, and I think we did have that feeling before," Annie said.

"Yes, that could have been enough with Margie. But Rolanda did seem to accept everyone else put at her table that we know of."

"But everyone wasn't Margie."

"Rolanda did want to run the table, I think. She thought Margie just asked to sit there without Management talking to Rolanda first from what I heard from Angie."

"They don't take our tablecloth away anymore," said Annie, thinking about how Management ran their table. "All they had to do was make the late dinner 15 minutes later."

"Yes," said Carolina, "That Manager would have been pulling our seats out from under us next. People can get so carried away in the dining room. Maybe that room is possessed."

They laughed again.

"Maybe we should hire the cook Lillian's family will hire part time," said Annie.

"Or that singer to sing 'Hound Dog' for us every day."

"He's coming back, I heard," said Annie.

"It won't be the same," said Carolina with a smile. "We always remember our first time."

Annie said, "My husband was my first time," but she looked surprised at what Carolina had said. That was exactly why Carolina had said it.

"Anyway, by the next time we see Boris, he'll be all acclimatized and Americanized. Wait and see. He'll sing only Russian folk songs and bore us to death."

"Or become an Elvis impersonator totally."

"Maybe we'll get someone suave and exciting at dinner for Lillian's seat," said Carolina.

"At our table?" said Annie. "Margie is as exciting as they come. Crazy is more like it."

"Do you mean us, Annie?"

"Hell, no. I mean everyone else."

"Well, good night. Remember to put the chain up when I leave if you aren't going to the movie."

Carolina made it to her apartment to think. She missed Apolonia. But there was a picnic planned for her Church for her to look forward to—they would be selling food at a booth at a local block party, ethnic foods like pirogues and funnel cakes. (It sounded like the Food Manager here might be running the food concessions for the whole block party.) She'd relax beforehand and hug her dog and cats at her friends' home where they lived.

Carolina dressed next morning in a brown and tan sweater set and tweed skirt with brogues. She looked ready for a walk in the country—the English countryside of the 1930's. She left for an enjoyable day, leaving her problems with the Buckingham Courte behind her. The cats and dog welcomed her as warmly as she could have wished. Penelope, her cat, was the only one who didn't come to Carolina when she called, making Carolina love her even more. Penelope often did the opposite of what humans wanted and she liked to be courted, which Carolina did. Carolina thought Penelope was the most loving one of all and so essentially cat. Carolina did secretly love her best of all. She loved them all and wanted to stay with them that day and forever. But work was good and working for charity was better, even if it was only cooking at a bazaar.

Carolina took her turn at the food booth, hoping the cooking oil wouldn't ruin her long treasured English country clothes. She had worn these since her parents were alive. (One finds connections wherever one can.)

A very handsome man in his 80s entered the booth, a new member of the congregation. Carolina perked up. Was he married? Did he travel? He was well groomed. (Was this a set-up from her friends?)

"Hello," he said. "My name is Gordon."

"My name is Carolina." Pause. (She noticed he did not say North or South.) "Are you new to the Church?"

"Yes, I joined after my wife died but didn't have time to come much at first. I needed new experiences to get me over the grief so decided to volunteer. It seems to be helping."

Carolina smiled.

The day was fun. Gordon was a hard worker, doing the heavy and dirty work with the friers, taking care of Carolina, who mostly served the food plated by Gordon and collected the food coupons and money.

No one came to relieve them. (It was a set-up.)

After they finally were relieved, they ate together at a booth by themselves and walked around the block party, playing games. Carolina felt like a girl again, winning a frog herself at a golf game and being given a giant gorilla won at a dart game by Gordon. He seemed to be approving. They walked to the cars after stowing some of the Church gear in the vans and donating the "prizes" they had won themselves. Carolina and Gordon found themselves still alone by the design of their companions.

Carolina asked if he had started spending time with women since his wife's death.

Gordon seemed surprised at the question but pleased at her forwardness.

"Not yet, but I suddenly seem ready." He stopped for a moment, getting ready to ask her something.

"Excellent," said Carolina quickly. "I know a wonderful woman, Rita, who would love to go out."

Gordon seemed disappointed and said with humor, "Speak for yourself, Carolina."

Carolina laughed and blushed.

"At least come to dinner at our place. The food is dreadful but no worse than you had today."

"With you or Rita?"

"All of us, spinsters and widows all. You said you were looking for new experiences."

"Fine, when?"

"Next week. We are losing Lillian, our friend, who is leaving the Courte and will have an empty spot at the table."

"What day and time and what kind of clothes do the men wear?"

"A week from tomorrow, 4:30, and Friday work casual. Come a little early, and I'll meet you in the lobby."

Gordon agreed and smiled in a half-embarrassed way. "I'll see you at Buckingham Courte with bells on."

Details were exchanged and farewells made.

Carolina got back to her apartment wondering what she had gotten herself into. Carolina had never played matchmaker in her life. Rita had to dress up. She needed a man and this one seemed dropped in front of her like the gentle rain from heaven. He was meant for Rita. He would marry her and take her to Europe on their honeymoon. Of course, the group would have to be careful and check him out.

Then Wanda happened to them.

CHAPTER SEVENTEEN—WANDA HAPPENS

Margie was slated to suffer once again in this world. She did seem to have that little rain cloud following her like the character in "Lil Abner," although Wanda was a trial to them all.

Wanda was a tough broad who spent her life using people. She was the kind to cow a daughter into meekly serving her day and night for the rest of her life. But somehow the daughter flew the coop because Wanda was there at the back table to bully them all. How does one say no to a woman with a walker AND on oxygen?

Oh, the oxygen. She would ask even Annie in her walker to pick up the heavy canister from the floor. It was always running on empty for some reason. She would ask all of them to turn it on, hook it up, switch dials, whatever, although they all said no, the first six times. She would ask a server to help her and be refused until she found one nice enough or stupid enough who would. They would turn dials and wait for the explosion that might come from pressure or from some mistake with the way they handled the oxygen tank. One could hear the sound of gas escaping, but that was not as frightening as the sudden silence when it stopped. The canisters made of heavy gray metal looked lethal somehow.

Rita simply ignored her after the first few of Wanda's emergencies. Dot did the same. Annie was the next to stand her ground. She had bent over and picked up the canisters once too often. She told Wanda that residents were not allowed to help with medical needs here. Even Carolina finally said she was not a nurse and couldn't accept that kind of medical responsibility. That left Margie who had little resistance to being pushed around, her husband having seen to that. Margie had been bullied all of her life. Wanda had aides she paid for part of the day, but they were not allowed in the dining room. Her aide had a way of disappearing, the way people do when they are being bullied for someone's emotional gratification more than for the help they can provide.

Dinner became a succession of orders for Margie. Wanda would smile in that phony, insinuating way of hers and say something like, "Margie, can you get my aide? I need my prescriptions. I can't find all of my pills."

Margie would leave her food and go to the library looking for Wanda's aide on duty. People would stare at her as she left. Servers would leave Margie's plates of food for her to eat, now cold, and shake their heads.

Wanda would make cell phone calls and receive them during dinner so there would be two loud conversations going on at the table to the annoyance of the other diners.

Wanda would sometimes tell Margie to get up and get things from Wanda's walker. She would (probably knowingly) mess up her dirty cell phone and ask Margie to fix it for her. She would ask her to scroll down and find a person's name during dinner, anything she could think of to treat Margie like a servant. How can you refuse a woman on oxygen? She was the snake and Margie the rat in her power.

Wanda knew Margie had an internet connection in her apartment and would ask her to bring all sorts of information for her to dinner. Margie had made the mistake of bringing her something that Wanda had said she was interested in one day. Then the request for something became daily. Margie looked trapped and felt humiliated but found no way to get out of it.

Once Wanda said her oxygen was out and she couldn't get her aide on the phone to come early. Would Margie go upstairs and get a canister for her? Margie didn't want to go into Wanda's room alone but she had to. Everyone watched as Margie left the dining room. Ike even asked her why she was leaving as she passed his chair, showing his disapproval of Wanda's treatment of her by shaking his head in disgust. Margie, nevertheless, went up to Wanda's apartment using the key Wanda had given her to pick out a full canister in a line of them along the bedroom wall. Margie was afraid of being accused of theft or something. She had reason to be paranoid after what had happened. Margie chose one and brought it down, the wrong one, of course, according to Wanda who sent her back up. Margie came down with the right one this time but not knowing how to exchange it for the empty one. Neither did Wanda or she pretended she didn't. Wanda got the whole table involved, even a server, as she showed them that the current bottle was on zero, and she needed oxygen immediately. She refused the offer of one of them to call 911. She said Margie could fix it. Finally, with Margie on her knees in front of her doing something she was told with the plastic attachment on one canister and with a server turning two dials on another, Wanda, waiting for the last moment she could milk without having to fall out of her chair to appear convincing, said she could feel oxygen through the plastic nose hose she wore all of the time. By that time, dessert was being served and Margie had not eaten anything else. (Wanda had, every course.)

Wanda worked the canister switching racket twice until even she realized she was pushing limits.

They all hated her. All of them. She would ask each of them to pull her up from her chair after eating. She would demand it of the servers after Margie realized it was not safe for her to do so.

First Wanda would follow Annie and Margie into the library, and then she'd insist that Margie keep her company after dinner every night in the library whether Annie was there or not. Wanda did this unless Wanda found better pickings between visitors or phone calls or other tables in the library to intrude upon, even if they had only one seat left and Margie was left embarrassingly stranded.

Carolina and Annie advised Margie not to do what Wanda told her to. They said to tell her she was a resident here as well as Wanda was, knowing Margie couldn't. Margie's defense was retreat. Margie began hiding in her room again.

Wanda was a master at what she did. She'd work on Carolina or Annie when Margie wasn't there. They all longed for Lillian to return with her, "This is NOT food!" again. It seemed each replacement they got for disliked diners who left was worse than the one before, although it didn't seem possible.

Wanda would ask them to read this or read that for her, although she could see perfectly well. (Having someone looking for her misplaced glasses was good for some laughs for her too.)

Everyone in the area watched the table with enjoyment in a perverse way, glad that Wanda wasn't put at their tables. Those at the table began to resent everyone in the dining room. Now Annie and Carolina knew there was something really wrong at the dining table and knew only too well what it was.

Dot at this time started to be vague, sometimes almost falling asleep at the table. Carolina and Annie thought it was a great way of escaping Wanda who knew it would do no good to ask Dot for anything.

Margie went knocking on Carolina's door one day. She needed to talk to someone. She said she had decided to move. She had to. She couldn't stand the dining room anymore. If it wasn't a Rolanda it would be a Wanda.

Carolina said it was time to take a stand—refuse.

Margie said, "But how can I? She's a sick woman. We're supposed to take care of the sick."

"She's a sick bully. She doesn't belong here. But you'll never be free of a bully until you learn to fight back. Make an excuse that you hurt your back. Use illness against her as a ploy as she does, if you can't be direct. Smile and fight her with her own weapons. We will support you."

Margie couldn't lie and remained a deserter from the table, eating alone in her room every night, cooking her own food, hiding from Wanda to get her mail and fearing a knock on the door to face Wanda in her walker asking for help with her oxygen.

A day came when Wanda was late for dinner.

Rita said, "She's probably late so we will be the last table to get served and ruin our dinner."

The server, Nova, came over and asked what they wanted to drink. Most were happy with water until dessert time.

"We'd like to order now," said Carolina. "It looks like the last dinner guest isn't coming down tonight."

"She called," said the server. "She's coming. You'll have to wait. I'll get that coke and more water for your table."

"Please bring rolls and butter if we have to wait so long," said Dot.

The tablemates made faces.

"I don't think it's fair that Margie stays in her room when she's paying for her meals. She's too scared of being criticized for asking that her meals be sent to her apartment. She's afraid of being a topic of concern at Management's morning meetings or being lectured to again by someone less than half her age," said Annie.

"What can we do?" asked Dot.

In some way, each woman seemed to brighten up and raise her head, like experiencing some visitation from the Holy Ghost. They laughed.

Annie asked, "Are we going to have some fun? By the way, does anyone have her cell phone with her?"

"I do, and I know what to do with it," said Rita.

Wanda came into the dining room. She looked with satisfaction that revealed to her dining companions, forced to eat with her, that she had planned that every table in the room be served before theirs. Everyone else was already on their entrees while their table sat there with bread and water.

Wanda was ready to get out of her walker and asked if someone at the table would assist her by moving the chair closer to her walker. If the person wasn't strong, there was a good possibility that they would both fall. One could tell she expected someone to help her. Her request was more of a command.

"You'll have to ask a server. I can't do that really; my doctor would be very angry," said Rita.

"We'll have to ask for more rolls. Rolls and water were all we got, waiting," said Dot.

"Did you think the rolls were more stale than usual today?" asked Annie.

"Yes," said Carolina, "definitely."

The server came back ready to take their orders. Wanda asked her for help sitting down. The server moved the chair while Wanda tried to hold onto her which Nova resisted. Wanda had to use the table and her walker for leverage.

"Will you put my oxygen tank next to my chair, dear?"

"We're not supposed to do that," but Nova reluctantly did.

Wanda knew from the response she'd gotten in general that she'd better not ask for help adjusting her canister, so she did whatever she had to do herself.

Entrée orders were given, and a request for more rolls.

A disgruntled Wanda asked, "When is Margie coming back? Why isn't she here?"

"We don't know," said Carolina. "Maybe she'll never come back. She talks about moving."

The rolls and salads came. Wanda asked that butter and rolls be held by the others in front of her as she used one hand to get them, her other hand seeming to become limp so she could annoy the others. The other women got the idea and simply put the condiments and requested items down in front of Wanda so she had to use two hands.

They started to eat in earnest. Of course Wanda got a phone call. She talked loudly into the sticky phone she never washed. Her hands were sticky too.

They heard her talking in her hoarse voice, probably that way from years of oxygen drying her throat and from smoking. She was talking to her aide.

"Can you come early, dear, to help me out of the dining room? I can't find a strong man around here....about 6:20...I'll get someone to come out to tell you when I am ready...Could you stop at the store and get some cinnamon rolls for me and some cigarettes?...I know I'm not supposed to smoke...Would you call Estella up and ask her to come an hour earlier tomorrow?...And tell her to get an extra canister from the agency, I may need an extra...She has to get her daughter to school first?...Tell her to get a sitter...I really need it..." (Then angrily) "She didn't tell me she wasn't coming anymore!...She has to give me notice...The replacement won't know what I need. Make sure I get that extra canister. I don't care how you do it!"

The other women at the table ate silently, hiding their smiles.

Wanda got off the phone and smiled her fake smile. "Did you hear that? You see how little I get for all of the money I spend. I see you've finished your entrees. Carolina, would you get the waitress over here so I can get my food heated up?"

"I'll gesture if she goes by."

She did not go by. Wanda looked around and saw another server going by. She yelled, "Girlie, girlie, would you get my plate heated? It's cold."

"I'll send your server over."

They all waited, but the inconvenience was felt most by Wanda.

Their server came back and got the plate heated. Wanda ate alone as the others, who had finished, waited.

The server came back bringing their desserts that they had ordered when she first took their order. She left Wanda's dessert by her entrée. She got coffee or tea for all of them. All but Wanda finished their dinners.

Rita pulled out her cell phone and tried to dial a number. It didn't work. She asked Wanda, "Will you check this number in my directory for me? I didn't bring my magnifying glass."

Wanda looked with outrage at her and said she didn't know how.

Wanda said she wanted ice cream with her pie. The server was busy clearing off another table for the next seating and wouldn't look at them. Wanda saw Milton leaving and yelled, "Milton, will you ask Nova to come over?"

He said, "Ok, if I run into her."

Nova came over and said, "I have to clear off your table, and I was told to take your tablecloth."

A flash of anger passed over Wanda's face. "Would you wrap up my pie and give me an extra piece to take with me?"

"I'm sorry, I can't. I can wrap up your food but can't give you extra to go, and there's no time for you to eat the extra pie. I can give you some cookies to take though,"

"OK, then. Will you go out and look for my aide to help me leave? I called her. She should be in the front of the dining room or in the lobby."

"No, I can't. I'll see if she's in the front, but I can't go looking for her. I have my work to do. The second seating is waiting. What's her name?"

The server came back saying no one of that name was there. She started to pick up the dishes to get the tablecloth.

Wanda turned to the other women. "Would you go for my aide?" looking at each woman there and missing the face of her willing puppy, Margie.

Carolina got up, getting Annie's walker. They all stood up but Wanda. "We'll send your aide in if we see her on our way out."

"Could you help me up and take me with you? Where are you going? I'd like to go to the library with you," Wanda said in an ingratiating way that was so obviously insincere.

They looked at each other and shook their heads no. "No one seems to be going there tonight."

"Can I come up to your room, Annie?" asked Wanda.

"Maybe another night, I'm expecting company."

"We'll tell the concierge you need help here if we don't see your aide." (They left and did indeed find her aide and sent her in.)

"That was rough," said Carolina.

"Tough love they call it," Annie replied.

"But we don't love her at all, do we?" asked Dot, rhetorically.

"I hope we love all souls in this world. We had to do it," said Carolina.

"She just can't treat people that way. We're complicit if we let her treat us that way," was Rita's comment.

Dot said, "She had no pity for Margie, did she? That was a good touch with the cell phone, Rita."

"I shuddered to think she might touch it and make it sticky."

They dispersed to their various apartments.

Wanda found the pickings rather slim for her games. She began to eat at a later seating, showing up for either on a whim, not an accepted practice. The Dining Room Manager talked to her about it, but it didn't help. Not with Wanda.

One day Wanda did not appear. She was gone. It turned out she had avoided signing a lease and went on to find someone else to bully in Texas on the Gulf Coast.

Margie came back but with a whipped look in her eyes, even worse than after prison. She looked like someone who had come out of a bunker after the bombs had fallen but with an air of shame about her for her cowardice.

One day in the lobby, Ike bumped into Annie and Margie. He said, "Where did you move to Margie?"

Margie said, "I'm still your next door neighbor. There are only three apartments occupied in that wing on that floor. We pass each other in the hall."

"Oh, I haven't noticed. I did notice your friend Wanda has gone."

Margie was crestfallen, more like cut down at the knees.

CHAPTER EIGHTEEN—DINNER WITH GORDON

Then there was the day Gordon came to dinner when Wanda was eating at the second seating. They had kept it a secret so she wouldn't come back. They all had to do some negotiating for a day they would all be there except Wanda. But the day came.

Everyone dressed up a bit, some lots more than usual. For some, make-up came out all dried up in old bottles or had to be borrowed or bought. Others had make-up galore. Rita had a make-up guaranteed not to highlight wrinkles or to make the skin look like spider webs, and it worked. Carolina wondered how they had ever survived their teen years and twenties with "dating" being so hard. Was it even fun? Tonight it was important to make Rita look good.

"Give her the good lines," Carolina told the others.

Carolina met Gordon at the front of the building. He was perfectly dressed, ironed, a lot too GQ for her taste, but Rita would love his clothes. Carolina was aware of the stares of surprise at seeing her with him. Gordon gave her roses in a vase so she wouldn't have to run around before dinner putting the flowers in water. She wanted to take them into the dining room. He had a bottle of wine for them too that he carried along with the flowers. Carolina was so happy to see him and not Wanda that she almost hugged him. At least that's what she hoped the reason was.

He escorted her into the dining room to the back table. She indicated "Wanda's" seat and put the flowers on a windowsill nearby so the view of each other at the table would not be obstructed by the flowers, beautiful and expensive as they were. Margie came in and then Dot with Annie. Dot wore something that looked like a bridesmaid's veil as much as anything else. Fashionably late, Rita entered in a Paris dress reminiscent of Audrey Hepburn in a wide skirt with a tight waist. Her hair was piled up on her head. She looked like an actress out of central casting rather than Audrey, an older version for the aging population. She overwhelmed the chair. She was the center of attention.

Everyone "ooohed" over the flowers. The server brought wine glasses for the wine which Gordon himself opened with theatrical panache and served. He expressed his luck at escorting five lovely ladies to dinner. Each of the women said nice things about him, common interests were found. Dot and Gordon liked Rex Stout's detective, Nero Wolfe. Annie and Gordon liked to watch baseball. Margie and Gordon watched shows about the Universe. Rita and Gordon bought the same liquors and luxury food items. Carolina and Gordon shared the Church, talking about the profits from the block party and what would be done next year.

They were all just having fun, having made up their minds to have a good time. Gordon talked about his beloved wife, asking if they had heard of her. She had been a singer of some local renown, singing at fairs and universities, even for a local public TV station in the County where they had lived.

Gordon said he was interested in selling his house. He asked about the Buckingham and good real estate companies they had used, and retirement and financial planners and things of that sort. He asked about the Buckingham. It sounded like he wanted to move in the place or at least settle in their circle of friends.

He seemed to be leaning a tiny bit towards Rita, her clothes and jewelry catching his attention, after all, he was a man and their eyes were caught by shiny, moving things.

Dinner was declared over by big pressure from the second seaters. All were satisfied. Dinner had been as perfect as it could be here; Gordon was perfect. They waited for the walker brigade to leave and Gordon escorted them out, carrying the flowers up to Carolina's apartment where she had drinks ready to serve for all of them.

They talked for hours. Before leaving, Gordon got their names, apartment numbers, and phone numbers, hinting that another party might be in the making. They got his phone and e-mail address info too, each of them on cards he handed out. They seemed like old fashioned visiting cards from another century and tasteful. They escorted him out and split up to go to their own apartments, Carolina accompanying Annie to hers.

Annie and Carolina started in together. "OK," each said as she sat down. "Something is wrong here." Both ended in laughter.

"But it can't be," said Carolina. "He's been vetted by the best—a police officer in my Church. Everything is right. They couldn't make such a big mistake. Gordon and his wife lived in that house for 20 years. He worked. He escorted her to her singing engagements. There's a picture of them in the local newspaper my friend looked up on microfilm. The neighbors liked him. He moved away for a while after his wife's death but came back to put the house up for sale, although it isn't as yet. He lives in a nice apartment around here with amenities, expensive.

Annie said, "He's a fake, maybe he always was or not. He is now."

"Let's tell the table not to date him separately. But we would hate to lose a great guy for Rita or even Margie."

"Margie!" said Annie. "Even God isn't that good."

"Now, Annie!" reproved Carolina.

Gordon came over to various apartments where they met as a group or went to community activities or even out to fancy restaurants where he paid. He asked each of them out. He tempted Rita with future plans to visit Europe and Broadway plays and restaurants. No one bit yet, afraid of violating Carolina's admonition not to date him separately or else not letting Carolina know. He just seemed to be a lonely man looking for companions. Rita seemed to be weakening. She'd stopped collecting stuff and looked in fashion magazines at designer clothes from Paris. Gordon seemed to be what he probably was, a fine looking distinguished man with great clothes. There were some of them out there, although the women had come to believe there were not from watching TV shows about predators and from hearing endless reports about men's perfidious behavior. Everyone had friends or family betrayed in some way by male family members or boyfriends. Did they expect Gordon, if he were genuine, to look like a drunken hobo? What is modern life coming to? He had no criminal record, no complaints filed by neighbors, a nice pension and investments.

Carolina had a thought. She was about to encourage Rita to date him. Rita was a bit shallow but Carolina knew that was mostly how men liked women. Margie or Annie would be the more amusing choices if Gordon were smart about women, and Carolina herself would make the sacrifice for Rita.

Just one more test, thought Carolina. She had thought of what Margie had said the other day about information being lost in black holes or maybe not. It was a hot scientific topic. It made her think that these days, with the loss of longtime neighborhoods, other information was lost. Where were Gordon's former in-laws?

The next day, Carolina dressed in her "working" clothes for sleuthing and went to the big public library where local newspapers were kept in paper form. She had a date and page her friend the policeman had seen in microfilm already. She found the paper copy in the basement in the Newspaper Archives of the main branch of the library. She found a Sunday supplement with a story of a beautiful woman with a beautiful voice. Her husband sat next to her. Unlike the old microfilm in black and white, the picture was clear, down to the last mole. Yes, that was interesting, she thought as she used her magnifying glass to check the mole that Gordon had on his neck. No, not there. The likeness was close, but on a clear color picture, one could see the Gordon they knew was not the Gordon in the picture. What could be easier than to find a man of good character one resembles, whose wife has died. Wait to see if he goes away. Maybe he dies naturally there. Maybe not. He disappears. One does some cosmetic work with dye and style and comes back, not too close to home, of course, since one's heart is broken. It's not hard to use someone's pristine and attractive background. One meets lots of women, picks out the rich ones, and goes from there. Old story. The women are easy pickings once they trust a man. Carolina was sure Gordon had checked the popular internet social networking sites to be sure there wasn't an available good shot of the real Gordon, and

Gordon picked a very old, vulnerable population to dupe. And even people who check identifications don't do DNA or fingerprint testing unless the person is being arrested. Carolina was overwhelmed that she had led her friends into danger.

Carolina talked to the Head Librarian and left with a big book of newspapers under her arm. She made an appointment with a detective and had a long talk. The book was left, as well as a description of a man named Gordon and a card with his fingerprints on it, the old fashioned visiting type card he had handed out. Suggestions were made to take Gordon's picture to another county where he had lived for identification and to find some of the real Gordon's relatives or those of his late wife.

Carolina left with a broken heart. She had to save her friends and other women, but the evil in people's hearts by choice was unbearable. She couldn't understand why people these days kept saying they made "mistakes" when they did awful things like deliberately killing or cheating someone. Mistakes are things you don't intend to do. "I didn't calculate right and the building fell down" is a mistake. "I grafted and didn't put enough cement in the structure" is not. We all make mistakes. The second is some sort of personal and even criminal violation. Carolina reminded herself to be resolute, although she knew again the temptation to fall into despair.

She was getting out of the taxi when Gordon met her at the Buckingham entrance. She hoped her face hadn't betrayed her. She asked why he was there.

"I'm taking Rita out," he said.

"Oh, where?"

"New York City."

"Have you been dating the women at our table?"

"Some. Didn't they tell you? You refused me, Carolina. You were first."

"I most certainly did not. I feel rejected, you know." She smiled. But she knew she was not prepared yet to engage in this battle of deception with Gordon, a consummate grifter, and he could tell immediately.

He smiled a rather evil smile. "I thought you might be too smart, Carolina. I can see you know. I may be a little smarter than you thought too."

"Annie and I saw through you the first night you came here."

"We're going to my car now. Do you understand? I can hurt you or one of the people here if you make a sound."

"It's too late, Gordon, or whatever your name is. The police know. Go. I'm not a good hostage. I'll slow you down and you don't need a local dead body."

"But I do need more time to get my belongings ready. I almost got into all of those nice investments your friends have here. Will you promise me one more night of freedom from the police? That's all I'd get anyway if I took you with me. I'd believe you if you promised, Carolina. You're the only person in the world I'd believe."

Suddenly, the fire alarm began going off; people started to come out. Margie ran up to Carolina and Gordon, spoiling their conversation.

"We were going out," said Gordon to Margie looking at Carolina meaningfully.

A fire engine came rumbling to a stop in front of them, the firefighters jumping off. An emergency vehicle was behind. Gordon lost his grip on Carolina and started to walk off hurriedly.

Carolina yelled, pointing, "Stop him! He molested me. Help!"

Two police officers took off and caught him near his car.

"Thank heavens," said Carolina. "He won't be going off to another group of women." She told the police to call the detective she'd talked to that day. Gordon morphed into a really ugly man. How could that be? He really was a chameleon.

Carolina looked at Margie. "Ready to go to the police station again?"

Margie looked like she needed a foxhole.

The next night Carolina gave an "Apology Party." She invited the table members to her apartment with handmade favors of praying hands. A tape was playing the song "What Can I Say After I say I'm Sorry?" A "Thank Heaven for Our Safety" banner was tacked up on the wall of her living room.

The five of them sat around her table as Carolina made a speech saying she should have been more careful about whom she brought around to meet them. They drank black coffee and a cake made in the shape of a crow with black icing.

Margie told the details of how Carolina had been saved. "I was hanging out in an empty apartment on the first floor with a window that jutted out. I had it opened to see if I could hear the people who hung out at the main entrance. You know how I hang out in apartments. I was sitting on the floor by the window when I heard what Gordon said to Carolina about taking her as a hostage. I wasn't eavesdropping. I was going to close the window since I'd heard enough noise to know the apartment wasn't for me. I knew I couldn't get out in time to get Carolina help and even shouting out might have caused him to run with her, so I pulled the fire alarm near the apartment in the hall. I know where they all are. Then I got to the front entrance to ask people to hurry out with me. You know how people usually congregate in the lobby before being made to go outside. That's why we were around Carolina so quickly."

Carolina hugged Margie again, glad they hadn't run away from the table after Margie got back from prison.

"Wait until we can tell Lillian when she visits. She will insist that she would never have been fooled," said Dot.

"Maybe not but he knew a lot about food, who knows?" said Annie.

"I have more to tell her and you," Carolina told the group. "The police have found the real Gordon on a trip in Brazil somewhere, so the fake Gordon might be a mere swindler. He was smart enough to be a great con man and not a murderer." She asked if any of them had been robbed in any way. Their "no's" satisfied her.

A relieved Carolina said good-bye, cleaned up from the party and put an end to that chapter. She remembered that her friends had told her that her own cat, Penelope, had been actively hostile to Gordon when he had visited them. Maybe she should bring Penelope here. She would use that test for men in the future as the need arose.

Carolina washed, gelled and waved her hair. She hated this procedure after all of these years of doing it over and over. She had to wait for it to dry before she could go to bed. She made plans to get one of those new permanent waves that she heard did not even get hot on your head. She thought about her friends today and ideas formed in her mind about what to do to help them, as she took the rods out of her hair and went to bed. She decided on no reading tonight. She grumpily lied to herself that she would NOT leave her apartment tonight if the fire alarm rang for another non-existent fire. The firefighters would have to carry her out in her nightgown if they wanted her to leave. She fell asleep thinking, "At least my hair will look good."

CHAPTER NINETEEN—CAROLINA WALKS AGAIN

Life continued on as before, the "Lillian chair" remaining empty, filled for a night by passers-by. They all wished it to remain that way, avoiding being stuck with the worst, and getting an interesting companion from time to time. But the gloom from before held.

Carolina said good night after dinner, ascertained that all would be in their apartments that night and prepared. She rested awhile, made notes, got out her heavy cane and left her apartment.

She walked directly to Annie's first. Annie was watching a game show. She and Carolina played along with the show for a bit, then Carolina asked Annie what she thought was still going on. Had something come to her yet?

"No," said Annie. "The man thing didn't work out, but I guess we should all let nature take its course. We just have to get used to being alone for now. I, at least, have great memories. I miss my home that was sold, but my children visit. My family is growing with great-grandkids. I'm OK as far as we all are with our fears of getting some disease we can't fight or losing our memories so we can't function."

"I guess that's enough," said Carolina.

Suddenly Annie covered an imaginary crystal ball in front of her, "I see a woman, she is saying...." Carolina had been entranced, believing some revelation would be coming forth until Annie stopped. Annie could always surprise Carolina with glimpses of her fun spirit that had dimmed in these later years. They were all dimmed in some way. Maybe it was just no fun here. They laughed anyway.

The phone rang. A woman who'd been like another daughter to Annie was calling from another state. Seeing Annie happily occupied, Carolina waved good-bye and left. She was glad to see Annie's door was on an automatic lock.

Carolina left to see Dot. Visiting Dot was always an experience. Dot answered, wearing a babushka type scarf like people wore in the Old Country or in *The Godfather*. Black, of course. She invited Carolina in and they sat on the couch. Carolina's conversation went right to Gordon. Had he bothered Dot in any way? (She had not had to ask Annie anything about that since Annie's family controlled her money and Annie was too smart to fall for a man like him.) "No," said Dot, "He came around. I think he saw I didn't have much money and I spent what I did have on my hats. He asked lots of questions about how my retirement fund was set up and about other people—their interests and such. Now I see where they were leading. He was looking for rich women and how to approach them."

She added, "Let me show you my new hats. I got some wonderful forms too."

They stood up. Carolina noticed how Dot wobbled getting to her walker. Dot never left her room without it, although she used furniture and a handrail to get around her apartment for short distances in the same room. The new hat stands were in the kitchen, making Carolina worry about fires, but Dot didn't cook much. The heads made of plastic, or some other clear material, looked like they'd been melted in production so the features ran together. They were scary. The hats on them were the black felt ones and the black veils she was now wearing to the dining room.

Carolina suggested moving them to another room for safety from a kitchen fire.

Dot said, "There's no more room anywhere else. I've heard of some shelves for forms that allow you to pile hats above each other, so I'll have more room. I'm saving money for them. They're sold mostly to stores for display."

"Good," said Carolina. "I like your church hats, the bright ones, better. They look more flattering on you, I think."

Carolina said good-bye without being escorted to the door as usual, but they parted smiling at each other.

Carolina passed Lillian's old apartment. So far life with three generations must be a success—as long as the food was good.

Carolina sighed going to Rita's apartment. She was let in by a woman who seemed to have something to hide, whose expensive clothes were wrinkled like she hadn't had them pressed. They sat down. Rita needed little encouragement to talk about how lonely she was. She could get around better than other people here. Why was she here? Probably her children thought she would meet more people and have more activities to participate in than in her home. They felt they were off the hook for visiting and checking on her all of time too.

"Have you looked into the activities here?" asked Carolina.

"Phyllis was right. Those Arts and Crafts activities are laughable for people over 6 and under 95."

"I know," said Carolina. "But there are card games and trips too. I'm sorry to hear how lonely you are. I've been my own family for most of my life since I left home, my own unit in society or whatever they call it. I miss my sister, but I never felt we were connected as a family making decisions together until she was so sick, and I took care of her. Now she's gone. I can't imagine how married people like you feel who've lost a partner in life."

Rita was crying. "It's so painful.

"What are you going to do about it?"

"I thought Gordon was interested in me. We met, you know, in New York."

"No, I didn't know until recently."

"We were making plans to travel. It happened very quickly."

"Did he take your money?"

"No, I stopped the check I'd just given him the day after he was arrested. My lawyers are taking care of my security issues. I'm all right there, I think."

"What else? Did he hurt you emotionally? Did you meet him at hotels?"

"Heavens, no! I'm not that kind of woman. He wanted to but I didn't. I might have on the ship. I just felt how good it was to be with a man again and now I can't live without it." Rita sobbed.

"My matchmaking days are over," said Carolina (with no Mr. Knightly for myself). "But there are ways to meet men, nice ones I'm sure. Of course Gordon was volunteering at my Church and had been checked out." (Maybe you should try going to bars, thought Carolina secretly.) "But you have to take chances if you want something valuable to happen to you. Senior Centers, maybe. The other women there can tell you what the man is like if you like one. Matchmaking online? But that's where Margie's ex is hunting. In the meantime, travel with a group. TCM, that movie station, gives a cruise with old-time movie stars. Go on that. You can afford to. If you stick around here, you'll meet old stick-in-the-mud men. Maybe a hot one will pop up but not likely. I mean men become widowers every day. There are groups for people who've lost their partners. Or you could volunteer at a hospital and comfort the new widowers there. I mean help them for real and let something good come out of a good deed if it happens naturally. At least you'll know they're not married and will have met their families. How about political volunteering? You can make phone calls. That's not too strenuous, and someone may have a grandfather on the loose they can introduce you to. The organization will give you the senior names to call maybe. Don't give up and don't be desperate. Have fun. You look great. But don't expect a smoothie like Gordon."

Rita sat higher and higher. She began to plan. She thought of things she'd liked to do and still could.

"I might just surprise you, Carolina, and move to Florida. I look pretty good in a bathing suit for my age."

"That's drastic. What will it do to our dining table?"

They laughed.

Carolina left, feeling better but guiltier than ever. Before she did, they talked about safety and men.

"Don't keep your activities a secret next time."

"I thought someone might be jealous. Why didn't you fall for him, Carolina, he was after you first."

"I was tempted, I must admit. To be honest, I was being generous. I wanted such a great man for you."

"Next time, try him out, Carolina, before you pass him on to me."

Appropriately humbled, Carolina smiled as she left.

Carolina steeled herself before she headed on to Margie.

Margie was eating ice cream. She asked Carolina if she wanted some. They ate. Apolonia came out to jump on Carolina's lap. She seemed to be following something with her eyes by the wall in a disconcerting way.

"I'm looking for another apartment or to move out. I don't know. Another State where the police don't take you away for no reason. And I still had to pay for my apartment and food while I was 'away.' Maybe I should move near my son in a hotel that will take pets even if he's not settled."

"What about your lease here?"

"Oh, that. I'll ask for a two month exit clause. God knows, I've had problems here that would kill an ordinary person. I've spent an awful lot here for nothing much."

"You have friends here."

"And enemies."

"It seems Rolanda had enemies. You just have people who don't understand you. We all have people who don't like us. Some people even think I'm a bit, uhm, on the preachy side. But what they think about cither of us isn't necessarily true."

"Then that Gordon, or whoever he was, came and fooled us."

"Not for long. You saved my life maybe. See how much you are needed here? Did anything happen with him?"

"No, I think he thought everything I had was tied up in the divorce. (See, my ex is good for something.) And I didn't want Gordon either. I was spared, but no thanks to him, like Emma was from Frank Churchill in Jane Austen's *Emma*. (There was that reference again.) Not that I'm a catch like Emma. Even my husband didn't want me."

"Now, Margie, you have to get over that. Lots of people get divorced now, even after long marriages. Men of certain ages sometimes do that—more than ever in this permissive age. Did you read Dreiser's *Sister Carrie*? Books like that help you understand people in everyday life as much as the ones about string theory. They are based on truth, the books that last at least."

"I'll match your Dreiser with a Hardy—Michael Henchard in *The Mayor of Casterbridge*, and raise you a Shakespeare—Malvolio in *Twelfth Night*."

Carolina laughed, "You win." She guessed she deserved that for being dense and preachy. It had been the teacher in her coming out. She'd forgotten that Margie was so well read, although it didn't seem to help her.

"I may move to Lillian's old apartment, but I'd have to sign a lease starting from that date. I'm all confused."

"Negotiate. Remember you're not alone. You can talk to me or Annie. We'll go with you to Management if you want."

Carolina left, going home. She felt no fear on this journey. No one was here to hurt her anymore. She got home to think about the best thing she could do. Poor Apolonia. What was disturbing that cat? Could one have an exorcism for a cat? She'd heard saging was good. But that was too New Agey for her. Perhaps Margie should move.

CHAPTER TWENTY—FINICULA

Carolina made phone calls the next day. A few days later she had a professional with her, waiting. One by one, the table friends came to her apartment, all except one.

They sat in a circle waiting expectantly. Carolina spoke, "I know what is wrong here, Annie, and you did see something. Do you remember?"

"No."

"You saw Dot's hats. They are getting gloomier and gloomier. Something is wrong with Dot. I visited her the other day, afraid Gordon had hurt her somehow. She was safe though, at least from him. She's lonely though. I think we may have caught her just in time before some tragedy. She doesn't have extra money for trips or to plan for a future she'd like, no one visits her. She can't even afford the hats she gets on e-Bay. We don't think about her much since she doesn't show the emotions we sometimes do. She was giving up, becoming gray with sorry looking work hats. Hats weren't enough. She took pain medications for her muscle pain, the reason she uses her walker. She was on oxycodone prescribed by a Doctor for a while, then began buying it from one of the workers here who she found was smoking something illicit in the empty apartments now and then. It's odd how people find each other when think they need to. He supplied her illegally as a favor and for some money to supply himself. A word has been said to him and he's stopped. He has since left, you may have noticed. There was no real evidence against him and Dot does not need the pressure of the police right now.

You saw another thing, Annie, that was really important and helped me to figure out what was wrong here. You saw Dot without her walker that day in the hall that seems so long ago when Rolanda died. Remember? The drugs actually helped her with the pain, and she was going for a walk outside to the park maybe for the first time without her walker. She didn't speak to us that day and we forgot about the incident with all that happened afterward. When I visited her in her apartment recently I saw what the drugs were doing to her. She was wobbly and depressed. She's getting into dangerous territory. We need to help Dot. Mrs. Phillips here is a professional, specializing in interventions. We have a plan."

The plan was implemented. Dot, with a cousin as family representative, agreed with them. As a result, Dot left them for some time.

Several months later, five people met around a dining table at the back of a big dining room, one wearing a hat in the shape of a "V"—a vintage victory hat in red, white and blue that those at the table had bought for her on eBay that someone had made for the end of WWII. Four of them read notes of gratitude and affection before them on the table. Dot had aced rehab, had a new doctor who prescribed appropriately for her and was better, although she still needed her walker. Dot had returned to the fold.

Carolina and the others talked about what having real friends meant to them. They were the same people here as before but their relationships with each other were so different.

Margie spoke, "I got another apartment. I don't want to leave here yet. When my son settles down, I will." Now even Margie sometimes changed her heartbroken tune to positive songs like Aretha and the Eurhythmics' "Sisters Are Doin' It for Themselves."

Rita said, "I have some cruising brochures. You all have to come to my apartment to see them soon." (She didn't tell them yet she was going to invite Dot to go with her on a short cruise at her expense which no one but her and Dot would ever know how it was paid for.)

They smiled.

Annie said she liked her new brand of detergent better than her old one. She gave a knowing glance to Carolina.

Carolina, Annie, Dot, Rita and Margie sat for a little time in silence appreciating life and each other. Carolina was satisfied that she'd finally gotten the people at her dinner table in order. The mystery of friendship in the hardest of circumstances was the mystery they had somehow solved. Hatred had been easier to understand.

Together they had "fixed" what was wrong here, at least at their table.

They ate their meal in contentment.

The new Dining Room Manager came over with her wheedling but iron-lady voice saying, "Hi, ladies. Tomorrow you're getting a new dinner companion, a woman. She has some problems, but I'm sure you'll welcome her as you usually do…"

THE END

ABOUT THE AUTHOR

 Helen Grochmal was born and raised in a coal town until sent by the Great Society of the 1960s to a small private college. After graduation, she worked in the civil service to pay her way through an M.A. in English from Penn State and an M.L.S. in Library Science from Rutgers. Then she worked as a professional librarian for over 20 years, ending her career as an associate professor at a state university in Pennsylvania. She began writing in her 60s, a memoir at first, then fiction. *MANNERS AND MURDER* is her first published work.

www.ingramcontent.com/pod-product-compliance
Lightning Source LLC
Chambersburg PA
CBHW020320260626
47156CB00004B/1306